Mr. Cl ~~~~

A Story b ~~~~

For Judy

*And for Madeline Jane Melton, fearless
maker of imaginary sandwiches*

1.

There's a little girl in here. In among the lines about puke and weird things to eat that might as well wind up being in it, and some other stuff that may be of similar interest to you, there's a little girl. That's something you should remember as best you can. It does take a while for her to actually be in it, but when it happens things more or less take off. That's the way it is with little girls.

Alice Elizabeth Jenkins was her name. Her whole name anyway. The one that got used on school mornings, when the PA system would say "Today's lunch is fish sticks, tater tots and some sort of a greenish yellow pudding. Alice Elizabeth Jenkins, report to the main office."

That was never good. It usually involved one of the assistant principals staring across the counter at her over a pile of tardy slips, or someone finding a slightly booby trapped toilet seat. Those had her name, so to speak, written all over them.

But we better begin with a few explanations. A few spinouts, you might say. You might even wind up saying this is actually loaded with them. Some people, some smartypantses, are already sitting around all juiced up to rip it to ribbons for that (among other things). It's gonna happen, you wait. But it's still a good place to begin. And boo on those people anyway. They just don't know how to party.

The first of the explanations is this. Some of you already know it, but East Texas in the summertime is hot. Really, really, hot. People have come up with sayings about Texas having two seasons, "Summer and January," and stuff of that nature, but the main thing to remember is that it's hot. You could check a thermometer if you had one, or a rock or just about anything, and the first thing you'd get is "you gotta be joking." That kinda hot. It's sticky, too, like watermelon juice all down your arm, but maybe we'll talk about that later. For now, just keep it in mind.

It also has a lot of pine trees. Pine trees are nice looking, and you can do some good things with the wood, but climbing them is a little worthless. You don't have much to get a grip on at first, and when you do you really wish you hadn't. You wind up covered with sap, dead sticks smack you all over and your shoes, or your feet, get all gadzooked for the effort. There's not much to see up there anyway, except for other pine trees, and all the pine cones you could ever want for making fake Thanksgiving turkeys are already laying around on the ground.

In case you haven't figured it out, that's where we are, East Texas. Really not a bad place to be in summer, if you're a kid. Adults tend to slow down and lean against anything shady (except the pine trees if they can avoid it). They also say "sheesh" a lot and wipe their foreheads with bandanas. But kids just pull on fewer clothes and run around like crazy.

2.

Explanations also involve a little bit of history, but don't worry: you won't really learn anything much. Anyway, around a hundred years ago, some people had gotten off a train near here after riding it to as far as they could afford. They gathered their bags and walked off, looking for a place to build homes and make a living. This was happening all over the western part of the country, and a lot of it was going on in Texas. Some of them wound up in what they call the Hill Country, where they cranked up oompah bands and began making some pretty good beer. Others went on out to West Texas, where they hunkered down against dust storms and waited for the oil boom. The people here chose a flat spot in the red dirt, although it did slope down to a creek on the north side and, partly because of that, had too many mosquitoes. They didn't think they were supposed to run west to east like this one, so later on they named it Crackers Creek. A couple of scouting parties went out to see if they could improve on things even just a little bit, but they were back in a couple of days with empty packs and more mosquito bites. "This," they said, "Is it."

So they began to build. After a couple of false starts (with some families throwing up their hands and moving to Dallas and Shreveport) and some squabbling over who got what and all of that, they actually came up with a pretty good little town. It had a school, a sawmill, a place that made shoes for mail order, some stores and a dance hall for weekends. Most everything was made of pine. Its first mayor ran for office without anybody running against him; the others figured they were too busy on the "making a living" part to pay much attention to the government. The mayor's name was Frank, and on his first day in office he leaned against the outside of their one-room Town Hall, ran his thumbs along his mayoral suspenders and announced that the town would be called Bernice after his mother (he didn't have a wife, which was one of the reasons he figured he had time to be mayor). The others had stopped what they were doing, cocked their heads to one side for a moment and then gone back to business. The paperwork got turned in to the state and that was all there ever was to it. The town grew a little, caught fire a little and got re-built and made better a little. But it always was, and as far as anyone can tell always will be, Bernice.

3.

There is another thing that needs explaining. Later on, you might consider it a little spooky, which always helps. The first person to really have what you would call a company in Bernice was Mr. Ambolini, who owned the shoe-making place ("You'll Amble Better In Ambolinis"). He was from the eastern side of the country, and goodness knows why he decided to make shoes in Texas. Maybe it was because his family was pretty crabby and demanding and he just needed to go. He brought his wife with him and they built a house in town near the shop.

Mrs. Ambolini had come from what you could call a high society family. She was willing to go with Mr. Ambolini wherever he wanted to, but when she had stepped off the train she thought they had reached the far, far edge of wherever. She had a pretty tough time adjusting.

One thing that helped her adjust were her tea parties. Back where she came from they called it "afternoon tea," and everything was just so. Here, it was pretty tough to make anything just so; you had to be happy with so-so, but that didn't stop her. She invited the neighbor ladies, who were mostly coffee drinkers. They showed up the first time expecting to be asked to volunteer for something. But Mrs. Ambolini just served tea and cookies and talked about developments in town and new movies and almost anything that, for a while, took her mind off the fact that the roof was leaking pretty bad in spots and they were having a problem with skunks.

After a while, the other ladies got the hang of it. They began to bring their own goodies – peach pies, kolaches the size of hub caps – and secretly shared copies of magazines like "Vogue" and "Redbook" so they could lead some of the conversation. Of course, there were still jeans to wash and kneecaps to bandage. Some of them also had paying jobs on top of all that. The ladies never totally got that stuff out of their heads. But for a couple of hours or so on Wednesday and Saturday afternoons, they could sit in Mrs. Ambolini's back yard under the trees drinking tea, fanning themselves and laughing a little.

Mrs. Ambolini thought they needed a little something extra, though. Something special. She sat there thinking about that one afternoon, spinning her parasol and nodding along to the conversation when it got on poison ivy and boy's baseball.

The other ladies didn't have parasols. They all wore sun bonnets with printed patterns on them. One of them, Mrs. McKee, had some pictures on hers that, when she looked close enough, made Mrs. Ambolini jump out of her chair. It was as if someone had popped her good with a dish rag. She excused herself properly, went in the house and phoned up Mr. Ambolini at work. She told him they were moving.

Mr. Ambolini stood at his desk, holding the phone in mid-air. He wasn't sure whether to slam it down or put it back to his ear and start yelling. Either way, he knew his wife well enough to know she had probably hung up.

Moving. It didn't appear they were leaving town, but the very idea burned him up. They already had a home. A decent enough home. Sure, if you looked close, you saw some walls that leaned a little, but they were in kind of a hurry back then and so what. He had also been concerned when Mrs. Ambolini had fallen asleep in front of the fire and her ball of knitting yarn started to wander around the living room like a croquet ball. But, again, so what. The plumbing could use a good going over, though, along with the wiring and just about anything else they could find someone to take a look at. But decent enough.

Mr. Ambolini burned up for the rest of the day. Then, as he was jerking on his coat to go home, he began to think, and the burning turned into kind of a smolder. He was a lucky guy to be going to see Mrs. Ambolini. She was pretty okay. She made crummy dumplings, and the noise from the back yard on Saturdays usually drove him off to go fishing or play dominoes, but pretty okay. He could talk to her about the business, or what passed for local bureaucracy, and she would answer back calmly unless he teed her off, when she treated him like he was a third grader who needed a little guidance. That was okay, too. Plus there was that stupid roof to mess with.

So he walked on home and went into the kitchen. Mrs. Ambolini was in there putting something together for dinner in a big pot. She turned and faced her husband with a look like "I know this is gonna be trouble but my mind's made up." That's a lot to look like all at once, but she had worked on it a bit. Mr. Ambolini put his coat on the back of a chair and walked over to her. He leaned against the counter and asked her what she had in mind.

4.

The Ambolinis took a lot of long drives in the country. On lots of those drives, they had crossed Crackers Creek and she had paid close attention to a hunk of land about 50 yards by 50 yards or so. On the front, it ran along the main road out of town and was bordered on the other two sides, away from the creek and the road, by pretty much nothing of interest. It probably had some water you could drill a well into and had just the right amount of pine trees; enough for some privacy, but not so much you'd go bananas waiting for a breeze. Most importantly, it would work for her little something extra.

So the building began again. Nobody could figure out who owned the land, which made that part easy. Next, Mr. Ambolini had seen lots of red rock houses on a vacation they had taken to the Ozarks, and he thought one would look nice near the creek. He figured out they should put it about 40 yards away in case it ever flooded, laid out a kind of a basic plan for which way it should aim (right smack at the road) and bought the rocks. They began to arrive on big trucks from Arkansas. At first, they were just laid in a big pile behind where the house was supposed to go. Then they found some guys in town who, being skilled at fibbing a bit, said they could whip up a nice house out of them and went to work.

As they did, the house began to develop some real character. Not the kind you read about; this was much worse. Or better, depending on how you looked at it. After the foundation was laid in the direction Mr. Ambolini wanted, he was smooth out of ideas. That didn't slow down the builders, who worked on each side of the house without caring much what the others were doing. The finished product looked from different angles like a gas station, or an English farmer's cottage, or a tiny castle that had been turned into a junkyard office. At night, it looked like a big rumply mastodon who had decided this was a good place to lay down and die.

The insides were not much better. Or, again, much worse. You walked in the front door and the first thing you thought was that you were headed into a haunted house. It was nothing but one little hallway for about fifteen feet, when you had to turn left and were dumped into the kitchen, which was big enough for a dining table and a sitting area by the fireplace. Behind that was the big bedroom, then a little one, then what you would call a study if maybe you wanted to learn about the plague or swamp creatures. There was also a bathroom and a few closets and, other than a shed with a dirt floor behind the house, that was it. Mr. Ambolini thought the finished product was odd, and it sure was, but Mrs. Ambolini couldn't care less. After the furniture was moved in, she spent a whole day walking around on the land by the creek and writing stuff down. Then she measured the rocks that were left over and wrote down some more stuff. Then, while Mr. Ambolini was still at work, she got busy making phone calls.

A few days later, a big truck pulled up on the road in front of the house. A couple of big guys got out, looking pretty confused. They checked the address again and then knocked on the door, expecting some kind of a troll to answer it. Instead, Mrs. Ambolini threw it open, blew past them with a smile and headed for the back of the truck. She pulled open the doors.

The insides were stuffed to the gills with pots of lily pads. There were a few tools, some mossy kind of dirt and other gardening junk, but mostly lily pads. They had survived the trip pretty well; a lot of them still had their flowers. Mrs. Ambolini started pulling out the pots to give them some air. The guys from the truck, Bud and Jimmy, pitched in and soon the driveway was covered with them. Then the building, as best you could call it, started up again.

Bud and Jimmy spent two days digging ponds, sleeping in a tent beside the road; Mrs. Ambolini had offered them the extra bedroom, but they felt creepy enough just going in for a drink of water. When they were finished, the land had three good sized ponds, all lined with the extra rocks and plastered with lily pads. In the end, they also decided to build sort of a baby pool right by the driveway. Then they looked around, grabbed their tools and the tent and tore out of there with a wave good-bye. They had lots of stories to tell back home about the wacky thing they had done.

Of course, Mr. Ambolini thought it was wacky, too. He pulled up in front of the house towards the end of the first day, turned a couple of shades of red while he kicked a few rocks and then took off for Ernie's Place to stew. While he was sitting there watching some other guys play cards, though, he thought up something. When everything was finished back at home, he went to a gas station on the edge of town that sold fishing gear and picked up ten dozen minnows. He spread them around in the ponds. Now he had his own personal bait shop. That's what he could say to his buddies. That made it alright, even if it was actually still wacky.

After spending a couple of days preening the ponds, Mrs. Ambolini invited the ladies over for Wednesday tea. They had to share rides, with some of them rumbling up on a hay wagon, but when they got a look at the lily pads they all agreed it was worth it. Mrs. Ambolini dragged a big box out of the shed and cracked it open. The ladies looked inside. Parasols. That really got them giggling. They each grabbed one, including Mrs. McKee, whose old sunbonnet printed with lily pads had started the whole thing. They spent the afternoon toodling around the ponds, practicing twirling their parasols and pointing at stuff. That was a good day.

They had lots of good days after that. Mrs. Ambolini made somewhat better dumplings, and Mr. Ambolini spent his evenings tending to the minnows. Sometimes he sang his best imitation of Italian opera to them, which might not have helped anything but didn't really hurt. He carried a few of them along with him on fishing trips, but secretly he still bought most of his bait at the gas station.

The ponds were a hit. People began planning their Sunday drives to include a spin past the creek, where they slowed down to look at them like farmers checking out each other's crops. Mrs. Ambolini always ran out and lassoed as many folks as she could, which was a fair amount, and served them pie and coffee while their kids zipped around trying to catch minnows with their shoes. Some college students from Stephen F. Austin even rode down in a big white bus, approaching the lily pads cautiously like they were gonna fly away, writing stuff in notebooks and conferring in serious little groups for a couple of hours. They got pie and lemonade. As Mrs. Ambolini herded them back to the bus, one of the students, a sophomore, took her aside and explained that these species of nymphaeaceae – really, that's what he said – were not able to grow in the environment that had been laid out for them. Mrs. Ambolini smiled a little bit, patted him on the wrist and pointed a long, bony finger back at the ponds, which by then were pouring over with nymphaewhatchamacallits. She then helped him get on the bus with an extra little slap on the rear. A pretty good little slap, actually. For some reason, that made her smile even more as she walked away.

5.

Remember, though, we're talking about history. That means things change. Sometimes it's no fun, and sometimes it's junk you don't even want to know about, but they do change. If it helps anything, remind yourselves that there's more pages for you to turn, and so naturally there's gonna be more fun. That's what we oughta be aiming for anyway.

So the Ambolinis died in 1928. That way they missed out on The Great Depression, which was no fun at all. They found Mr. Ambolini at his desk in front of drawings of what you would nowadays call the Spring Line. Mrs. Ambolini wanted an early morning funeral, and she wanted him buried on their land, so they dug a grave under the pine trees behind the house and gathered at sunrise for the service. When it was over, Mrs. Ambolini asked everyone to catch all the minnows and take them home. She felt she wouldn't have time to look after them.

Mrs. Ambolini did get some of the ladies to look after the lily pads for a while. Then she got on the train and went back East for a visit. She thought she might end up staying there, but everyone she knew seemed too busy for her and, of course, she missed her patch of dirt and her weird house. She came back and spent the summer tending the ponds, holding more tea parties and sitting in the morning sun by Mr. Ambolini's grave. One day when fall rolled around she raked up the leaves, cleaned out the fireplace a little and laid down for a nap. And that was where they found her, wrapped up in a blanket with a shiny new frog statue sitting beside her. The ladies buried her next to Mr. Ambolini and threw a nice tea party, but it didn't quite seem the same and soon they lost interest. The ponds began to show signs of not being looked after: the rocks started to slide apart and weeds began filling in the cracks.

The Ambolini's eastern relatives really never had any interest in the ponds at all. Other than paying the taxes on the land, they left them alone. They had an idea of where Texas was, and they knew the Ambolinis had left them some sort of a house and the factory. They also knew the factory made good money even in the Depression, since lots of people had lost their jobs and were trying to sell shoes. The money they were plenty interested in: they chose up sides and got banks and lawyers and figured out how to start a fight over it that continues to this day. None of that ever mattered to the people who actually made the shoes; it just meant a few more men with bow ties and sour faces passed through Mr. Ambolini's old office.

The lily pads did their best to carry on. For a little while, it seemed they might be gonna make it. But another thing about Texas is that it can be awful stingy with rain, so the ponds started to dry out. Things were looking pretty bad until Mrs. McKee gathered them up and farmed most of them out to the rest of the ladies. The McKees ran the auto parts store, so they gave one away in a paper cup with every set of spark plugs. Nowadays, their lily pad great-great grandchildren and assorted relatives fill fake plastic waterfalls, oak barrels and stuff all over Bernice. But the ponds themselves went to absolute snot. They looked to be a good place for three-ring mud wrestling (fortunately, no one had ever heard of that). The rocks went whichever way the mood took them, where they squatted down and got covered with vines.

When they ran out of rocks, the vines headed for the house, which had begun to develop all sorts of legends. For instance about how Mr. Ambolini went off his rocker one night, yelling "bad pot roast, bad pot roast" and chasing his wife through the house with a wooden mallet. No one pointed out that it would take about six and a half seconds to chase her through the house twice. Nor did they ask any questions about Mrs. Ambolini's legendary love of tarantulas, for whom she had built a tiny apartment building and sat, night after night, waiting for someone to knock on the door and volunteer to be tarantula food. Somehow nobody had mentioned the apartments when they had cleaned out the house. But it didn't matter; the legends grew and grew until Mr. Ambolini had itty bitty horns growing out of his head and Mrs. Ambolini made magic potions over the fireplace.

Now mind you, these were what you would call secret legends. No one over fourteen or so could ever be told about them. Anyone older would, of course, laugh the storyteller right out of town. But that's just because they wouldn't understand. To the legend keepers, the stories just got more understandable as the years went by. They sat in the dark on the kitchen floor of the Ambolini's old house (it never had a lock on it), shining flashlights on their chins and sharing new stories about the ponds having been built to raise miniature dragons and all. This usually built to a screaming point, with the kids running for the hallway, where they bashed into each other and then ran out the door.

One of those kids was usually the little girl. She had brown hair, bare feet and, usually, overalls. Her name on these and most other non-PA occasions was just Allie. And now you're all explained up. It still won't seem that way, and it was a long way to go to begin, but you are.

6.

Allie was born in 1962 and had just turned thirteen. She had lived her whole life with her parents, her little brother Butch and her dustmop of a dog in Bernice, where she had lots of friends and zero enemies. She was lucky that way. She was lucky most ways.

The first time you looked at the dog, though, you might not think so. Once you got close enough to figure out which way he was facing, a sort of aroma hit you pretty good. Kind of like the deadest end of a ditch mixed in with a couple pounds of catfish dough. He had an apologetic little underbite, though, and he could run like the dickens. He had shown up at the door of Allie's garage on a rainy night shivering from the cold, with a look that said "I got no place else to go." Allie and Butch had shut the garage and wiped him down good with some of her dad's shop rags. That wasn't really the best of ideas, because as soon as he dried out a little the smell really got going. It got so bad their mom cracked the kitchen door a dab to see what in the world was happening. Then she shut it extra good. Turned out that was the dog's best defense; he smelled so rotten a grown-up couldn't get near enough to boot him out.

It also turned out that, in fact, he had plenty of places to go. He was happy enough being Allie's dog, but there always seemed to be a new adventure over the horizon. The bad thing was that, for a critter his size, "over the horizon" meant under the fence. Allie's dad tried to keep up with him for a while, putting down bricks and boards and stuff, but finally he figured out how to fix the situation by cutting out a dog door (really just a square hole) in the fence. That looked a little strange to the neighbors at first, but once they saw him skittering off, heading out to patrol the dump or goof around with his pals, it made perfect sense.

The name that best befit him came to Allie as he was tearing across the yard one day on his way to a mud bath. She went to the hardware store, bought a red dog collar and ordered a name tag. On the form for the tag she put his new name:

SKEDADDLE

Then she put her name and phone number and one more thing she thought might save his biscuits in case some adults, holding their noses in teams or something, ever had a reason to read it:

SORRY ABOUT THAT

It was kind of hard to get his whole name out while he was still in ear shot, so they mostly just called him Skee. Butch had bought his mom a bottle of perfume for 99 cents at the drug store for her birthday, and she was surprisingly happy to let them use it on him any time they wanted. So, after washing him down every couple of weeks or so and using plenty of Lava soap, they would spray him all over with it. That made him smell like a fancy French ditch for a while; maybe a little too fancy. The other dogs laughed a bit, but he just stuck out his lower jaw even more and kept right on chugging. He knew he was a lucky dog.

7.

But we better get going. On this particular day in May, Allie was counting mud puddles. It wasn't that counting by itself was something she really enjoyed, especially since school had got out that day for the summer and she was ready to have some fun. No, Allie was counting them because she was the Official Sort Of Weather Girl for 327 Apple Butter Lane where she lived. Without Allie's constant monitoring, her family would be lacking in what she felt was an important piece of the local news. And she sure didn't want that.

You might say that Allie's way of counting them was a little different. She was not so concerned with actual numbers, or location, or anything which might interest a normal follower of the weather. What she was after was quality. A truly great mud puddle, one with character and style, was the color of chocolate milk and there was no way to see the bottom. That meant that when she smashed her bike tire right in the middle – which, you see, was her way of field testing puddles and most other things – there was always the chance that a frog or a snake would jump out or that she would be swallowed up completely. This added an element of risk which she felt was necessary for a true weather girl.

She had seen lots of television reports during hurricanes where she thought the weather people had wimped out just a bit. They would be yammering away at the tops of their lungs while palm trees and fire plugs went lopping by when, just at what they thought was the last possible moment, they'd say "Well Jim, I better get on out of here before it gets any worse." Allie thought it would be pretty cool if it got a lot worse. She could see herself flying like a windsock from a light pole for the cameras until her last pinky couldn't hold any more, then squealing as she splatted against the side of a sound truck. As they loaded her into an ambulance, she'd grab the microphone and say "I shoulda stuck with puddles."

Puddles could be pretty hard on a bike, though. Let's talk about that for a little bit.

Two Christmases ago, Allie and Butch had run through the house just a little curious to see what might be under the tree. Their parents were following behind them, moving a little slower. That was because their kids had already turned on the radio in the kitchen and then zoomed into their room to announce that there was light in the sky and it was time to get on their robes. Allie's mom had rolled over, looked out the window and then looked at the alarm clock. She then informed them that it was 2:57 and they had better turn off the radio and wish their biggest of all Christmas wishes that she could get back to sleep.

It must've worked, at least well enough for there to still be presents under the tree when they finally got there. Butch got a Mr. Disastro chemistry set which had all sorts of warnings on it that he had better be real careful because if not it could blow up. This made him especially happy. He also got some binoculars, a bunch of pajamas and a bag of rocks out of the creek from Allie. She had seen great potential in them for his polishing machine (the machine itself lived in a hole under a board in the backyard so the noise wouldn't make their parents loopy).

Allie got a new pair of wafflestompers, a Baby I Can Spit Up On Myself and a coat from her grandmother. Butch gave her a slightly worn copy of "Moby Dick" which they started getting calls on from the library a couple of weeks later.

But the most beautiful thing of all, the shiniest example of what the holidays were supposed to mean at least in commercials, was Allie's new bicycle. It was just one of bajillions that Santa Claus had parked all over the world that night, but it was special to her. It had a glittery white banana seat, a basket laced with plastic flowers and a misguided goose of a horn. On its sides it said "Pretty Little Princess." And, of course, it was pink as all get out.

Allie gave it a good enough test ride on Christmas Day. She rode it over to her friend P.J.'s house, then took it down to her school and paraded it around on the basketball court just in case anyone was watching. She rode it home and wiped it down good with a wet rag, then stood back just looking at it. After a while, she pushed it around to the shed behind the house and went in to watch basketball with her dad. Of course, she was back about eight minutes later, still just looking.

That night, Allie got out a pen and some green paper and wrote a letter to Santa while her parents were next door at the Anderson's annual holiday party. They called it "Noggin' Back Another One," and sometimes it got pretty loud. Allie used the quiet time to thank Santa for the doll and all the other good junk she got, and to thank him for all that Butch had got, too, because his handwriting still resembled somewhere a stork had been putting out a cigar. While she was at it, she wrote about her mom's bracelet and her dad's copy of "Red Rose Speedway;" although these had been her gifts to them, she thanked him for the chance to earn the money by raking up pretty much every leaf on the block. Finally, and in the best words she could think of, she thanked him over and over for her new bicycle, putting down a list of everything about it that was great as if Santa couldn't remember a thing. She figured he'd had a rough night.

Allie ran the letter out to the mailbox, double checked to be sure the stamp was nailed down good and plopped it in. From next door she could hear polka music through an open window. Someone was standing on the front porch over there trying to get rid of the hiccups in a dignified manner. She got a flashlight and went out to the shed, shining the light on the handlebars and the flowers, running her hand along the seat and promising herself that nothing was ever, ever gonna happen to it.

She then proceeded, over about the next three weeks, to beat the living crud out of it.

8.

Crackers Creek had some good bike trails on the north side, where it didn't slope so much. They were full of roots and rocks and pretty muddy, but all the kids spent plenty of time goofing around on them. Allie knew some short cuts through the bushes, so she won lots of races while school was out for the holidays. Skee rode along in the basket for a while, barking out directions and keeping an eye peeled for the competition. After the bottom of it fell out, mostly due to him being a ball of slime from head to toe, he just ran along beside her.

Pretty Little Princess got a lot less princessy real fast. The horn dangled from the handlebars, the front fender got bent up as if it were a shot at modern art and the seat started to split sideways. The wheels sprawled out all over the place when you sat down, and the nice pink paint looked like lipstick that had been put on in a tornado.

Allie's father walked the bike into the garage one night. He pushed down on the seat and watched the wheels go wobbling every which way. He spent a little time messing with it and wondering if they should get her another bike. Yeah, that would last about another month. So, when he got home the next night, he backed his pickup up to the garage and pulled out a bunch of iron bars and plates and stuff that he had found at work. Allie's dad was a good welder. He spent the evening duct taping the seat and adding all kinds of doodads to the bike wherever it needed it, which was pretty much all over. When he was done, he called Allie out to take a look.

Her parents had a record that had a picture on the cover of a big metal armadillo with tank treads. It seemed that was what her dad had in mind for the transformation. The front fork resembled a post hole digger, and from there it just got bigger and nastier. It took a little while to get it going down the road because of the extra weight, but once you did all that momentum made it unstoppable. Allie gave her dad a big hug and then, when he went inside, she climbed up onto the back of his pickup and pulled the bike up. She took a good look around, turned it upside down and grabbed it by the wheels. She picked it up, let out a little bleat and threw it onto their dirt driveway for all she was worth.

The bike didn't so much bounce as dig in good. The handlebars, which now resembled big ice cream scoops for Kung Fu Death With Raspberry Swirlies, grabbed onto the driveway. The rest of the bike flew up a little ways, then clumbered back down and landed on the seat. The whole thing just stood there on its head, giving her a look of "so what's next?" Allie crossed her arms and smirked a satisfied little smirk. She had some ideas.

But there was still the color to deal with. The name was a goner, wiped out by whanging through blackberry bushes and spinning out on gravel roads: one side said "et le cess" and the other no longer said a thing. So the next day, Allie got some masking tape from her mom's special drawer in the kitchen and covered up the wheels and pedals and all good with old newspaper. She spread the last of the paper out in the front yard and rolled the bike onto it. In the garage she found some old cans of spray paint; one black, one brown and a couple of what appeared from the lids to be disco camouflage. Allie walked back outside and jiggled the cans for a while. She popped the top off one, closed her left eye both for accuracy and fear, and let it rip.

When you're a kid, it often seems the best way to deal with a mistake is to dig deeper fast. Somewhere under the surface, maybe way, way under, could be some sort of a cure. Most of Allie's records, for example, had skips from being whizzed across the room at her brother, so she kept a nail by the record player to gouge out little hunks of vinyl. That made the needle go "padump" and land somewhere else; hopefully just past the problem, but not always. For years, her friends thought a guy named Bobby Sherman had a song about losing his chimp.

This was that way. As soon as she got started painting the bike, it developed lots of mistaken little droops and dribbles that were awful hard to keep up with. She kept spraying like she was fighting a fire; in a way, she sorta was. The first can of paint turned out to be maroon, but it didn't last that long. Next was a can of lizard green, which as you can imagine didn't really mix in with maroon too well. The bike was a rolling ad for blowing your nose.

Brown was next. There was a lot of that. It calmed things down just a little, but it wasn't until she started with the black that she was able to breathe normally again. Black was what it needed. The paint still sagged a little, but she worked it into little streaks with what was left of the classified ads and gave it one more good coat. She had just enough left over to put "BUTCH IS A POOP" on a piece of plywood and stick it on a tree limb where everyone could see it, but too high for him to reach; that way, when her parents came outside to yell at her about the sign, there was a chance they'd overlook the bike curdling in the yard.

She did have a hard time thinking up a new name. It was nowhere near a princess any more, that was for sure. Not even one of her mean old sisters. But she got an idea. One Saturday night last summer her family had all sprawled out in the living room to watch a scary movie. She and Butch spent most of it huddled under a blanket covering their ears; they fell asleep right after the popcorn was gone. Allie woke up later on because her parents were laughing at a commercial with some dancing elephants. The sound those elephants made was close to unspellable, but it summed up the bike pretty well. She got a little brush and some red model paint from the workbench and wrote it on the sides in big letters:

FNORRT. And that was that.

9.

Allie rode Fnorrt along her regular puddle route, kind of disappointed in the results. The most dependable ones were down to about half a tank, and most of them were bone dry. She had to circle around again to get properly spattered with goo.

She pulled up at the stop sign on Cedar Street to let the football team go by on the last of their spring training runs. All the guys knew her pretty well and waved hello as they huffed past. Allie was a big fan; she sold pennants at the games for 75 cents, and if somebody didn't buy one they got a bark full of sewer breath from Skee.

The football team had a name. We better talk about that too. The smartypantsed ones gotta earn their keep.

10.

After the Korean War – Bernice was always a little behind the times – they had a population boom due to the shoe company hiring more people. It got big enough to be called a factory; when you asked somebody where they worked, they mostly said "the factory," and you just knew. The boom, which was really a mild thud, got the town to thinking about high school football. They already had track and basketball for both boys and girls, but (again, as you may already know) football is big in Texas, and so they put down a field in the middle of the track stadium, added some more bleachers, ordered some pads and stuff and sat down to think about a school mascot. Just "Bernice" was an okay enough name for the other sports, but football was different.

Of course, it had to start with a "B" because of Bernice. That was pretty much understood. But what? Bears? Badgers? There had surely been a few of them wandering around the area at one time; there might still be. Bison? They had probably passed through until the heat and the mosquitoes had sent them trundling north. The more they thought – Bumblebees, Barracudas – the more they felt lost in the woods.

Then one of the gym teachers – she also taught health and ran the girl's track team – came up with a plan. They needed a few new hurdles for the track, and some starting blocks, so why not raffle off the right to name the team? They could whip up some spaghetti at 3 bucks a plate and sell tickets for a dollar or two, then have a fundraising dinner and announce the name of the pride of the town.

Posters went up all over. You'd think a carnival was coming through. The Name The Team contest was a huge success, and on the big night the gym was packed to the rafters. After dinner and some dining music by the local dance band, Les And The Miserables (the bass player read a lot and had a sense of humor), the school principal Mr. Padgett had stood up from his seat on the stage and waved around for everyone to be quiet. He spent the next few moments dealing with microphone feedback, fumbling around while everybody groaned, then reached into a bingo hopper to pull out the winning ticket.

Mr. Padgett looked at the ticket for a good little while. He turned it over and examined both sides carefully. Then he moved back from the microphone and motioned for the assistant principal and the future football coaches, who were also sitting up there, to join him in a huddle at the back of the stage. He showed them the name.

One of the coaches let out a snort. A couple laughed a little. The assistant principal looked around bewildered, pretending to be searching for his glasses. Or maybe a back door. They got to talking pretty fast, still keeping the volume down. Mr. Padgett motioned for the head English teacher, Mrs. Rathbunn, to come on up. Mrs. Rathbunn had been to a fancy college, so he figured she might be of some help. She informed them that the name wasn't obscene, or really even profane, and from what she had been reading they might have a problem with denying someone, Lord knows who, their First Amendment rights to free speech or something. Besides, it was the winning ticket, and rules were rules. Mrs. Rathbunn was big on rules.

Mr. Padgett broke up the huddle. The coaches and the rest just kind of stood around in the back. He stepped up to the microphone and announced, pretty muffledy, the name:

The Boogers. The Bernice Boogers. At least it started with a B.

The gym got even quieter. The drummer for the Miserables, who had been putting his stuff away, almost dropped a cymbal. Then most of the little kids – all of them, really – started laughing their heads off. Their mothers tried to shush them, which didn't work, and a few of the older ladies acted as if they'd just been shown something dirty. They sorta had, but the cat was officially out of the bag. Some of them, and all of the men, wanted to stand up and give a rip-snorting speech like something from the Old Testament to protest the heck out of whatever this was. But they didn't. They just stared at their empty plates and mouthed the name over and over. Boogers.

Oddly enough, whoever had won didn't jump up in the air waving their arms. No one ever found out who it was. It may have been the same person who, later that night, had snuck out to the "Welcome To Bernice" sign that stood by the edge of town and hung another one under it, one that said "Home Of The Boogers. No Foolin'."

The name, however, didn't stop the boys from coming to tryouts. Most of them even had a pretty good laugh about it, calling each other by their new moniker. "Hey, Booger." "How's it going, Booger?" At first, the coaches didn't pay attention to any of it. They still stubbornly called themselves "Bernice," which frankly was hard enough on a football team. Either way, they were able to field a good-sized squad; some of them had to play what you call both ways, which means on offense and defense, but secretly that just made them feel special. "Special" might not be a word they used with the other guys, but there you are.

Being a Booger meant you had to get tough. Real tough, real fast. Their fight song was "A Boy Named Sue;" if you haven't heard it, you need to. They put together a pep band to sit in the stands and play it at the games; they tried marching, but when they set foot on the field with all the majesty they could muster they just formed a sort of a curly-cue with a drum set at the end. Later on, after it got popular, they also had a dance team, The Bouncing Boogerettes, and of course they always had plenty of cheerleaders.

The cheerleaders had to make the big paper sign for the team to run through before the game. It took them a while to get the hang of it. For the first game, it said "ROLL BIG BOOGERS," which even from the announcer's booth looked disgusting. For homecoming it said "FIGHT BOOGERS," which seemed pretty pointless. So, for the next couple of games, it was just a big purple sign (the team's colors were purple and blue) with nothing on it. Then one of the cheerleaders figured out that they could just poke fun at the opponent's name (the other schools had already figured that one out), and the problem was solved.

The team started winning some games. The name probably helped; you would be closing in on the fullback to smack him hard for a loss, then see B·O·O·G·E·R·S on his jersey and think "maybe I'll let this one go for a few yards." They didn't bother with putting their last names on their backs, just the team's name again, so it had kind of a coming-and-going effect. Texas colleges, mostly the smaller ones, started to notice; their head coaches, looking back on a disappointing season, would call up their assistants and say "get me a bunch of Boogers." One of the players, a skinny kid with feet like run over pizzas, even made it to Texas A&M as the third-string kicker, and half the town, including Allie, had piled into school buses for the drive down to his first game. Hardly any of them got into the stadium, and he never made it on the field, but it didn't matter. They just hung around the buses, watching the game on a battery-powered TV and yelling "Boogers, Boogers, Boogers." That was a little confusing to the other team's fans, but the A&M people understood and joined right in. They knew about the Boogers. And so do you.

11.

After the last of the team went by, Allie finished her ride and pulled up to the house. She parked Fnorrt by a little green bucket near the garden hose. She filled the bucket with water and sloshed most of it all over the bike. Then she held her nose and sloshed the rest all over her.

Allie's mom came out with a towel and handed it over. She sat down on the steps and had a good look at her daughter, who was streaked in gritty Texas mud from her hair all the way to her toes. She was wearing an old Jefferson Airplane t-shirt she had found on the beach near her Grandma Betsy's and her blue jeans were held together by patches and holes. But, as you can guess, she was beautiful to her mom.

She was one of those pictures from baking sections in magazines, the kind where the caption oughta read "Don't Even Think About Starting In On This Because You'll Just Botch It Up." Allie looked up at her mom and smiled. "We're gonna need some rain," she said.

The next day was Saturday. Allie watched cartoons while her mom packed her a lunch. She was going on a ride with some other kids out to her friend Candy's farm to see some newborn piglets. Her mom handed her a sack full of her favorite sandwiches – grape jelly and mashed circus peanuts – along with a water jug and a dollar for some eggs from Candy's mom. Then she did some math in her head on just how many of them stood a chance of making it home and gave her another dollar. Allie stuffed it all in her backpack.

She rolled Fnorrt out to the street and waited with her pack on. In a couple of minutes up came Missy and Frodo; his real name was Felix, but the Hobbit books were really popular a while ago (they still were) and that was the price he paid for having gigantic hairy feet. He liked Frodo better anyway.

They headed for the farm, talking about comic books and records and other good junk for a while. Frodo's family was going to someplace in Colorado called Estes Park for vacation, so they talked about that, too. The sun started to smash down on them on the dusty road. It was a good, wide-open start to the summer.

Allie slowed down as they got close to the creek. The others rode on ahead, yelling back at her to catch up. Finally, they had to pull up and wait. She was stopped in the middle of the road with her head craned over her left shoulder. She watched something for a minute, then waved for them to go on without her. Missy started to ride back, thinking there was some sort of trouble, but then Frodo said something to her and they took off.

There wasn't any trouble. She was, in fact, looking at the funniest thing she thought she had ever seen. And that Allie, boy, she had seen some funny stuff.

One time her parents took her and her friend Billy to Henderson for a carnival. The last thing they did was get on the Ferris wheel, where on about the third go-round Billy barfed up an entire paper skewer of cotton candy. It wasn't real funny at the time, especially since some got on Allie's tennis shoes, but nowadays it was hilarious. She had also seen Skee, feeling he was not getting enough attention from Allie's dad while he potted some geraniums, latch onto his pants and tug until they were down around his ankles. That got him some attention, you bet. And it was Skee – who else – who came running into the yard one day with a half a chicken in his mouth, still smoking from a barbecue pit. He uncovered Butch's rock polisher, dropped it in the hole and then tried to blend into the way, way back corner of the fence for a couple of hours. Allie drew some pictures of a chicken and put up FOUND signs around the neighborhood, but after a while she figured it would take too much explaining. Plus she wasn't really sure you could hose off chicken, so she took them down. With all due respect to somebody's lunch, that was pretty funny too. But this took the cake.

Over in front of the Ambolini's house was a guy. He had his back to her, so he didn't know she was watching what he was doing. What he was doing was the funny part. He was hunched over the ground with his legs splayed out sideways. From that position, he was whacking at decades worth of weeds with what appeared to be all his might. Allie could see that he was using a machete, the same thing her dad used to chop up kindling. Every time he finished cutting through a clump, he scooted forward and started again. He was singing something in Spanish to keep the beat; when he got to "aREEba," he gave them an extra good whack.

He stopped and rested on his haunches. At that particular moment, Skee, who had toddered up behind Allie without her sniffing it, let out a bark. The guy peered over at them, kind of startled, then ran through a quick mental checklist of just how ridiculous he must look. He grinned.

After a few adjustments, he stood up and walked toward them. He was tall and pretty skinny. To Allie he looked to be between 70 and 100 or so. He was wearing a checkered work shirt and grass-stained jeans tucked into his boots. He stopped at the Ambolinis' old picnic table and ran the machete into a green canvas holster. "Come on over," he said.

Butch was still at the time in his life where you didn't talk to strangers; Allie, however, had advanced to the point where, at least in Bernice, there really weren't any. She rolled Fnorrt down the driveway and got off. The guy walked up, wiped his hand on his shirt a little and held it out. "I'm Charlie Sanders," he said. Allie shook his hand good. "I'm Allie," she said back. "Jenkins." Then, as usual, she got down to business. "What in the name of Pete are you doing?" Pete was apparently someone her grandfather knew; he always put the question that way to Allie. She figured Mr. Charlie, being kinda old, probably knew him, too.

We sort of skipped over something, which shouldn't really come as a big surprise. In this part of the country, and maybe where you live, something happens to guys, the normal non-teacher types, just about when they turn 21. At that point, any new kid they talk with usually calls them "Mr. (Insert First Name Here)." It's not always out of respect, because some people over 21 are downright nutty. It's really just a way of indexing them, of saying "Won't Play Tetherball With You But Might Give You A Ride If You Need One." Ladies are "Miss (Same Deal)," even if they are 93, have hairs shooting out of their ears and have been married four times.

Mr. Charlie leaned back a little and glanced over his shoulder. Weeds and rusty cans were scattered all around. "Well, it's the only thing I could find to work with," he said. "When I was in World War Two, our ship went through the Panama Canal to get to the Pacific Ocean. There were a bunch of workers in a line, cutting the grass that way. They were singing something I couldn't remember, so I had to make do."

"No," Allie said, waving her arms around to take in the ponds, the pine trees and the house. "What are you doing *here*?"

"Here," Mr. Charlie said, "is home." He smiled at her a second, patted Skee on the head - a sense of smell was not Mr. Charlie's strong suit - and turned to get back to work.

Allie stood there, a little stunned. For her whole life, or at least since she was old enough to start exploring, she felt the Ambolini place belonged to the kids. In addition to all the storytelling, it was sort of a stage stop for wandering youth. Now here was this guy, saying that he lived there. It probably meant the end of the legends.

Mr. Charlie looked back over his shoulder. He could see Allie's mind was stuck. He sat down at the picnic table and pointed for her to sit down across from him. Allie leaned her bike against the table and straddled one of the benches. Skee stretched out in the weeds for a minute, then wandered over to what was left of the ponds, grubbing around for night crawlers or something else horrendous.

"See," Mr. Charlie began, "I used to live in Texarkana. It's not too far north of here." Allie knew that; on the counter in her kitchen sat a picture of her and her brother holding hands across the state line that ran down the middle of the big Post Office. They had been through there plenty of times on their way to go camping and fishing, too.

Mr. Charlie looked down at the table. "After the war, I came back to live with my parents and look for a job. I even went to college long enough to teach for a while, at a little town not far away from there. Mostly English and girl's basketball."

Allie brightened up a little. "I play basketball," she said. "I always beat my Dad at 21. My folks say I'm pretty good."

Mr. Charlie smiled at her. "I'll bet you are. We'll have to play sometime." Allie glanced under the table at his boots, which were smeared with dried out mud. "I got some better shoes for it," he said. "Anyway, people started to move away from the town, so the school shut down. I needed a new job, so I bought into the Texarkana movie theater and learned how to run it. I peeled gum off seats, cleaned out the popcorn machine and finally moved up to where I was running the projector. I did that for a whole lot of years."

Skee came flobbering back holding something dried out and wrinkled between his teeth. He knew Allie would try to take it away from him, so he ran around to the side of the house where he could perform experiments on it in peace.

Mr. Charlie watched him go. Allie watched Mr. Charlie, still a little afraid he might say "now git off my land" or something else mean, even though he had invited her and didn't seem at all to be that kind of guy. You just never knew about people. It had happened once, when they were flying kites on Mr. Hansen's cotton field (he was one of the ones you didn't use a first name on). His old hound dog Snoddle had put on a show of trying to catch them for about halfway across the field, where he just rolled over on his back and started swatting at grasshoppers.

Allie noticed her pack lying on the bench and remembered her lunch. Maybe something good to eat would help sway Mr. Charlie's opinion. She got the sack out, took out the sandwiches and handed one to him.

Mr. Charlie was pretty trusting, especially when it came to free sandwiches. He took it out of the wrapper and had a big bite without inspecting it. For the next half a minute or so, it seemed to Allie that he looked like a distressed camel. He swallowed hard, put the sandwich back in the paper and pushed it way across the table. "For later," he said. He rolled up his hands, perched them on his knees and said "Do you want some coffee?"

12.

The thing of it was, Allie really didn't. She had tried some of her Dad's coffee a few times mixed with lots of milk and sugar. No matter what, she still couldn't kill the taste. It was nothing but fire ants and floor wax. But she spun herself off the bench and followed Mr. Charlie into the house.

Not much had changed in there in the past few days. The last time she was inside, they had played with an old Ouija board that someone's sister had left behind when she went off to college. The only thing they had was the board. That and a vague idea that it was supposed to grant wishes or something, so they took turns pushing a Nehi bottle cap around the letters, spelling out words like MINI BIKE and MILLION BUCKS, then sitting quietly for a minute to see if anything happened. The bottle cap had been kicked into a corner of the room out of frustration, but Mr. Charlie had nailed the board itself on the wall to cover up a grungy sort of mildew stain by the front door. So it did have a purpose, after all.

Mr. Charlie scooted a couple of dust nettles off the kitchen counter, then reached on top of a little green stove for a tin coffee maker. He took out the basket, rubbed it out some with his handkerchief and filled it with coffee from a red bag. He poured in some water from a plastic jug, jangled the pot back together, set it on the stove and turned on the fire. Then he got to talking again.

"After a while, people stopped coming to the movies downtown. They built one of those theaters with lots of screens out on the Dallas highway. Kids figured out they could sneak into most of two or three movies in one afternoon, and no one wanted to mess with parking anymore. So I sold my share at a loss and figured I was retired."

"That was kinda tough to take. I started driving around all over the place. I went to Florida for a while to go fishing, then I wound up in New Mexico on what they called a commune. I was way, way older than the rest, so they put me in charge of what was supposed to be the building detail. The most I could get them to do was push a bunch of hay bales together and then sit around waiting for dinner, so I came home."

The coffee pot began to gurgle. A kind of thick brown goo started lapping at the little glass doohickey on the top. Mr. Charlie didn't seem concerned; he sat down on an old crate by the fireplace, propped his feet up and stared into the ashes Mrs. Ambolini had missed. It looked to Allie as if he was, for the first time, bringing his life for the past couple of years, and the strange path that had brought him here, into some sort of focus. That was alright with her.

"No one I really knew back there was much fun. They were all busy spoiling their grandkids" – he shot her a sideways kind of a smile – "or playing afternoon bridge. I started to get antsy again."

"I was sitting in a cafe one morning reading the sports when I saw an ad for this place."

"For Sale: half an acre with house, shed and water in Bernice. Fronts on dirt road and sidles up to creek. Has ponds of sorts. Surrounding countryside full of fishing holes and assorted fauna. No take backs. Contact County Assessor's Office."

See, the Eastern Ambolinis had finally let it go. It wasn't a matter of money; they still had plenty of that. The simple fact was, they just forgot. The county had never had to bother with mailing out notices that people were behind on their taxes; there was always enough squawking around dinner tables and such over having to pay them that the money just kind of trickled in. So, when somebody finally checked, they saw that the Ambolini place was in arrears to the tune of about 900 bucks. They held an auction on the steps of Town Hall one day at the stroke of noon, but nobody showed up. The lady who was supposed to sell it thought she saw somebody pull in a few doors down, so she abandoned her post and ran over to point them in the right direction. It was a guy selling toothbrushes to the drug store.

For a while it seemed they were stuck with it. They thought about making it into a playground or something, but the thought of cleaning out the ponds and filling them in gave Merle, the county maintenance guy, nightmares about quicksand. So he took some of his own pool playing money and ran the ad in the Texarkana paper, figuring that a decent night's sleep was better than a couple of extra games with the guys.

"They didn't want much for it," Mr. Charlie said. "I could kinda see why on my first trip down here. But I took out most of my money and bought it."

The coffee was going full throttle. A burning rubber smell filled the kitchen. That seemed to be the cue for Mr. Charlie to get rolling again. He grabbed a couple of old mugs and filled them with melted tire. He handed one to Allie and gave her a kind of a "cheers" with the other.

This was it. No milk, no sugar, just eight ounces of piping hot gunk to pour down her throat. She winced a little and took a tug.

Mr. Charlie fumbled around with the stove for a moment, then turned back and saw that Allie was staring at a space on the floor. This was because she was pretty sure the top of her head was going to land there at any moment. That was something she had to see. The rest of her raggly body was sizzling with little electric shocks. She looked up at Mr. Charlie. "Mmmmm," she said.

He wasn't fooled. He reached into a cardboard box and pulled out a can of condensed milk, opened it up and poured a dollop into her coffee. That kept her head screwed on, although her right leg still doodled around a bit.

They headed back out the front door with their mugs. Mr. Charlie quieted down again, walking around in the yard and thinking to himself in a "we can put that over there" kind of fashion. He found an old tennis ball nesting in some tall grass and threw it to

Allie. Skee came back around the corner, looking satisfied with his testing; for reasons of national security, he had eaten the final results. After a while, Missy and Frodo rolled up and short introductions were made (they figured they could pump Allie for information on the ride home). Mr. Charlie followed them around the place for a while, being shown all sorts of insider secrets, including where the Webelos used to camp and the mashed-down place in the floor of the shed where somebody who had just watched "The Great Escape" had started to dig a tunnel to the creek (he had to stop when his mom found all the dirt he had stuffed into his jeans; otherwise, who knows?). After leading him through a round or two of "99 Bottles of Beer" back at their bikes and yelling around for Skee (who was already off on his next secret mission), it was time to go.

13.

Allie filled them in some on the way back, about how Mr. Charlie had been in the Navy and knew how to run movies and spent time working for the communists in Mexico. She was pretty excited. When they split up in front of her house, she did kind of a running departure off of Fnorrt and took out for the door. Before the bike had even crashed into the wood pile, Allie and her backpack were in the kitchen bouncing up and down. She blabbered on and on about Mr. Charlie while her mother made dinner and nodded in agreement. When her dad got home, she followed him into the bedroom and told him most of the same stuff while he changed shirts and put his pocket junk on the dresser. Her dad smiled and peeled off Allie's backpack. He carried it down the hall and dumped it on her bed.

Butch slept in the middle bedroom. He was in there trying to smoosh one of those felt bouncy-dog heads you see in the rear windows of cars onto an old toy dinosaur. It wasn't going well. Allie got the bobbly gizmo out of the head for him, stuck it on and roped it all together good with duct tape. He then spent the quiet time before dinner terrorizing his dad with Fidosaurus around the edges of his paper.

After they ate, Allie's dad listened to a baseball game while her mom read to Butch from his favorite old Robin Hood comic book. Butch could never understand why Robin didn't cut loose on the sheriff with some grenades and artillery, so she always worked it into the story somehow. Butch helped by biting the ends off the grenades and reloading for her from his machine gun nest on her lap while she boomed and peeowed herself silly. It was quite a show.

Allie watched it all from a slumped position on the couch. Underneath the sound from the radio and all the gunplay, something was bothering her. For a while, she dinked around on the floor with her marbles and a deck of cards, setting up little houses and then bowling them over. She watched the late weather with her folks and then got into bed. Night was closing things down.

After a while, Allie sat up and ooched her legs over the edge of the bed. She could tell everyone else was asleep; they were all making noises no one with even the tiniest bit of pride would make otherwise. It was time.

She got down, pattered through the house and opened the door to the garage. She found the light switch with her hand, closed the door and flicked the light on just long enough to visualize a plan; head for the garage door, miss the trash cans, raise open the door, grab Fnorrt and, for a little while, gone. Once again, not the greatest of ideas, and maybe even a bad one, but it was still pretty early and Allie did just fine in the dark.

It was a cool night. Skee and the others were over at the grain elevator conducting doggie drag races. Allie could hear a car radio playing by the football field. When she got near Mr. Charlie's, she jumped off the bike and walked it into the yard. In the skinny moonlight, Allie found a good long stick. She pushed open the door and let herself in.

The floor was cold on her feet. She had to feel her way down the hall and across the kitchen. Mr. Charlie was back sitting by the fireplace. She moved over behind him and raised up the stick. Then she whacked him in the shoulder.

Things have a way of going one way or the other. There are times when they roll along and unfold, and times when they run right off the tracks. Too bad for some of you, this turned out to be one of the rolling along times. Mr. Charlie had heard Allie's tires on the road and her hands on the door. He saw a flicker of her raising up and stiffened just enough to lessen the blow. It still stung a little, but he spun around and watched her quietly in the light from the window. It was pretty clear she wanted his attention, so she might as well have it.

Allie lowered her proddling stick to half-mast and inched closer to him. She put a hand on the chair and asked.

"What are you really doing here?"

Mr. Charlie looked at the ceiling. "Change," and maybe "escape," ran through his mind along with a few other words. Those would take some talking about. But here was a strangely courageous little girl loose on the town in her pajamas, and he knew she needed to get home. So, for the time being, he got down to business too.

"Goldfish," he said. "I'm gonna sell goldfish."

14.

We seem to have turned some kind of a corner. It happens a lot, if you think about it. Seasons have corners, school has corners and sometimes even friendships have them. Most of the time it feels like a floor you just finished sweeping; at first you'd rather have been playing kickball, but the end result looks pretty good and now there's something bright and new ahead.

This was all new to Allie. Kind of interruptive, too. She had plans to build a clubhouse in the backyard that summer, and maybe learn to shoot a bow and arrow better or play tennis. And figure out a way to make Butch disappear for good without people noticing. But now she had an unexpected, kinda crumpled up project. Mr. Charlie. And, to hear him tell it, his goldfish.

In the morning she pulled on some brown overalls and a Boogers t-shirt. Before she even got into the kitchen, she could hear a familiar noise. A combined motherly wailing and a call and response sort of screeching from her son. They were rehashing his daily visit from The Splatter Lizards.

Now, The Splatter Lizards were fast. And also completely invisible to everyone but him. Their goal in life was to have him wear at least one meal a day, and sometimes two. This time it was instant oatmeal with raisins. He sat in his chair at the table, propped up on a Houston phone book with crusty pools of it on his shirt and his face, whimpering and pointing to the heater grate where the lizards had run off to after tumping it over on him. They were singing

"Way Down Yonder In The Cornfield" as they ran, also in a register that only he could hear. That just made it worse. His mom was wiping gook off the table and the floor. She was listening to his squealy explanations and trying not to start sobbing.

Allie had little involvement with the lizards. She figured as long as they kept coming around she could get away with a whole boatload of stuff. So she took a couple of symbolic swipes at the mess with a paper towel, grabbed an apple out of the bowl, winked at her mom and hit the road.

If you're keeping score, that was the sticky part.

Candy had ridden into town to catch crawdads out of a putrid pond with some of their friends. Their normal methods using old bacon and nets and little dams had gone nowhere, so they were just standing in the mud flailing around like spider monkeys. Allie gave them a sympathetic little shout as she rode by. She headed for Mr. Charlie's.

He looked to be nowhere around. She walked down to the creek, thinking maybe he was taking a dip or something, then came back and took her first long look at his car.

Lots of fighting ships made it through the Second World War. Some got tangled up in later wars, some got sold for scrap and some just faded away. Mr. Charlie's car looked like someone had taken some pieces of the faded away ships and stuck a last salvo of silliness together.

It had rolled off the showroom floor as a 1964 Plymouth Belvedere; now there was nothing anybody would really want to show anybody else. It had a lot of unpolished chrome, four beat up doors and a mighty big hood. The insides were decked out in splintered plastic seat covers. Mr. Charlie had just laid an old musty blanket over his side of the splinters; some were poking their heads through like Marines getting ready for a final charge up the hill.

At some point in the past it had been a really regal gold color. That was all over. There were some here and there patches of a goldish tone, but mostly Mr. Charlie had sprayed it down good with gray primer. The trip to Florida had taken its toll, leaving gaping rusty wounds all around the bottom, so one afternoon Mr. Charlie had set some beer down on his driveway, taken some pink body goop and patched them up as best he could. Doing that right takes a lot more than an afternoon, and a lot less to drink, so the car just looked like it had been rolled through a bunch of fish flavored frosting.

To Allie there would have been no point in towing it somewhere and abandoning it any place but a sarcastic museum, so she figured it probably still ran. And run it did. It cornered worse than a tug boat, and the dashboard lights were blown to heaven, but on boring nights Mr. Charlie would take it for a spin on the roads out of Texarkana, playing an old silver spotlight plugged into the cigarette lighter – one of the last remaining luxuries - along the front panel to be sure he kept the speed down and singing to a radio sitting on the seat beside him.

Allie remembered she had gotten a tetanus shot for the start of school last year, so she glazed her hand along the trunk and went inside the house. Still no Mr. Charlie. She walked over to the counter, grabbed some bread and whomped herself up a mustard and onion sandwich. She carried it over to the fireplace, sat down and waited.

There are words adults use when they don't think kids are anywhere near the area.

You've probably heard them. Allie sure had. Her dad had let some fly once when he had jammed a screwdriver into the back of his hand fixing her brother's hamster cage. Butch had stared up at him with his big eyes and repeated, as innocently as you can, every last one of them. From then on, her father took a long look around no matter how much he was hurting.

Now a whole slough of those words came storming from the bathroom. Mr. Charlie had gathered up a bunch of ancient toilet paper cores and brushes and stuff and was carrying them out of there when he stubbed his big toe on the sink real good. All the old bathroom fixings came skittering out onto the hall floor like some juggler's poorest of performances. Mr. Charlie kicked at them a little with his unstubbed foot, reaching back through a lot of tarnation-type words Allie actually hadn't heard before. She guessed they were still pretty awful.

Allie took a chomp out of her sandwich and coughed a little. She sat there watching Mr. Charlie with a kindly kind of a "cluck" in her own big eyes. The old man saw her and got completely flummoxed. He shut his trap and looked at the floor. Then he took one more kick at all his mess, knocking it back towards the other rooms, poured some tar into his coffee mug and sat down beside her.

There wasn't much to say. Between last night's visitation and her showing up today unannounced, Mr. Charlie seemed to know Allie had decided she was in it for the day's haul. He probably would have advised against it, to say the least, but she hadn't asked, which said a lot right there. So enough of that. You probably saw it coming anyway.

Allie walked over and cut the apple in two. She gave him half. Mr. Charlie skirted around the embarrassment of all his naughty words by humming nonsensically while they finished. He threw his half a core into the trash and said "Let's do it."

15.

Absolutely no shoemaker's elves at all had stopped by the ponds the night before. They were just as ghastly as ever. People say gravity isn't the strongest of forces (and how would they know anyway), but you sure couldn't tell by what 50 plus years of it had done to them. They were a moonscape of madness all set about with some seriously scrubby fever trees. And now they were Mr. Charlie's problem. He walked over to the first one, set his jaw and turned back to Allie. "Get the tools out," he said, nodding to the shed.

She didn't see much point, unless Mr. Charlie had stuffed a bulldozer in there. But she went in and grabbed the hoes and rakes and sat them down next to him while he stood staring at what lay before them, wondering if it was too late to bolt and run. The last thing she found was pretty heavy, but she waggled it out and was pulling it across the yard when Mr. Charlie walked up and stopped her. "That, my dear," he said, "is an anvil. Won't do us much good."

Allie left it sitting on the ground and walked away with him. She thought they could use it to somehow break up the stubborn rocks, or maybe anchor Skee down so he didn't get underfoot. But Mr. Charlie seemed to already have a plan.

Hard work is supposed to be its own reward; at least that's what some people say. But they're probably the ones with the dopey opinions about gravity. In the summer sun on a Texas afternoon, hard work is just that. A lot of it is necessary, and some is kind of noble, but it's derned hard. For a girl with visions of snow cones dancing in her head, and a guy who really only had about a third of a plan, it was derned harder. That's about half a nugget of a naughty word, but it fits. Just don't blurt it out in Sunday school.

They wound up hauling for four days. Allie severed all the kudzu and dug up the trees and the geegaws Mrs. Ambolini had collected. Mr. Charlie moved the rocks back into place around the ponds and put down some plastic liners from the trunk of his car. They sweat through everything they had on and then some, taking their jungly riverboat of a task on towards some ultimate destination. At the end of each day, Mr. Charlie gave Allie a glass of warm soda from a big bottle while they calmed down a little. All those chemicals kept her moving on Fnorrt just enough to get home, where she gave her folks a grim report on the day's proceedings, gulped down some leftovers and then slid into bed. Once in the night Butch threw up about a bucket of candy corn blended in with bunny milk, but she was way too tired to get up and snicker.

The final result was pretty presentable; maybe not lily pad presentable, but right up there. Most of the rocks had regained some of their original slabby luster, and you could toodle around the ponds once again without getting your shoes all matted down with stickle burrs. Mr. Charlie stuck a few of the fallen statues back in the ponds, some cherubs who didn't seem to care they were coming out of their undies and the like, until they had them sort of a watery miniature golf course. Only there was no water. It hadn't rained in a good long while, and the creek water was fairly suspect even if there was a way to horse it in. So Mr. Charlie sailed into town in his carboat and bought a big black gardeny type hose. He figured out how to hook it up to the well and stood there for an extra couple of days, moistening the underbelly of the ponds and checking for leaks. Allie just waited beside him for most of that time, yelling at her friends out on the bike trails and doing some serious shovel leaning to rest her feet and her sizzling legs. The other kids kept sticking their noses in, cackling at the little angel asses – there goes a whole one – and trying to sneak through the gate. Mr. Charlie kept them at bay in a cheery "now git" fashion, tossing dirt clods their way and stomping his feet in a sort of a Russian tango across the yard.

Finally Allie couldn't hold her tongue. "They're gonna have to find out sooner or later," she said. Mr. Charlie splooshed some water on a gnarled unicorn. "Yeah," he said back, "but not just yet. You and me have some talking to do."

16.

Mr. Charlie had a lot of suits that weren't very strong; getting girls of any age to pay attention to him was just about foremost on the list. He was a little perplexed by how good Allie had suddenly become at standing around watching nothing whatsoever. He needed to do something highly unusual to shake her out of it and, with any more luck, get her to remember what he had to tell her. He thought about chaining her to the anvil for a while, but that fed right in to her current state of affairs. So he went into the shed and grabbed what you call a tow sack, a big burlappy thing with a wide open top, and carried it over to where she still stood. "Get in," he said.

Allie looked up at him with a persimmony smile. From all that she already knew about Mr. Charlie, this was sure to give both of them some experience. She climbed into the bag and held on to the rim like she was getting ready to hop along in a race. But Mr. Charlie put his hand on top of her head and shoved her right down in it. He put a knot in the end and hauled her over to the tickle tongue tree by the driveway. There he left her.

It was plenty hot in the sack. Allie was all pooched up like an earwig, smelling the burlap and trying to look out through the holes. She heard Mr. Charlie clanging around in the shed some. She also heard a few bikes go by on the road, but decided to lay low. She didn't want to miss whatever came next.

What came next was that she was lifted up into the tree by a rope. Mr. Charlie tied it off on a branch so she dangled around like a piñata. He gave the bag a good twirl and strolled off to finish filling the ponds. He kept walking by and butting her around, which is not nearly as naughty a word as you think. The third time he did Allie thought about urping a little, just to show she was really involved, but nothing good came out and it just made her dizzy.

Allie's dad pulled up out on the road. He had gotten off work early for the dentist and thought maybe he could take her to the house. He spotted Fnorrt leaning against the fence and looked over at Mr. Charlie. They had shared waves at each other aplenty, which around there was all it really took to feel like you knew somebody. Mr. Charlie sheeped a look at the ground and pointed at the sack. Her dad whumped his steering wheel, looked over at the vacant lot across the way and then just drove off. Maybe he didn't know either of them all that well. Not when you got them together.

Mr. Charlie got the ponds into the outer realms of waterdom and approached the tree. He spent a second pretending to sprinkle it and then he turned the hose on the bag.

One of his actual strong suits was the ability to put on a maniacal laugh. He gacked and screeched and soaked the bag and had a general good time for a few minutes while Allie sputtered and picked wet stringy gook from her teeth. Then Mr. Charlie stood back and decided he was done. If all that didn't get her paying attention, he might as well hang it up.

He sat down by the bag, crossed his legs and picked at the trunk of the tree. "This place will need about a human and a half to run it," he said. "I have to make a couple more trips back home to get the rest of my gear and say goodbye to folks. For all that time and more someone needs to operate the hose and such. I could use the help."

Allie really thought she was gonna urp this time. All she'd ever had responsibility for was doing some chunks of her homework and keeping the grass mostly mowed around the house. Her parents had started to leave her with Butch while they went to the dances, but she figured that was their problem and a little self-reliance was good for him. There was the time he had made himself some dinner out of a whole box of cornflakes and a bowl of mayonnaise, but it was still good for him. Other than that, no one had ever asked her to do much she hadn't done for herself.

She wormed her knees up to her chin in the bag, getting kind of uncomfortable. That was appropriate. "There's nobody else around I feel like I really know good enough yet," Mr. Charlie went on, "and the adults have their own stuff to do so far as I can see. Also I don't have nothing to pay." He picked off a low lying tickle tongue twig.

(Those like-lettered phrase phenomenons probably are turning out totally tiresome. There's a word for them we don't need to bother with. Some folks whose pants may be not all that smart say they're popular with our target audience, though, so for their sake try to put up with them. This has to come close to succeeding at something, even if it's something stringily stupid.)

He stuck a sliver of it on top of his tongue. "There might be a little money later on," he smacked, "but for now I got nothing to give. I could pick you up most mornings, share some of my lunch and try to get you home," he said, "but not much else of nothing."

Mr. Charlie winced a little at the taste of the tickle tongue. He left the whole proposition, as far as it went, right there. He thought she might figure it out and start squealing like she'd just been named Eraser Cleaning Kid of The Year at school or something, but that didn't happen. Wadded up inside the bag all steamy and sore, Allie was considering a handful of things. Her parents would be alright with it, she was sure of that. Her Mom had learned how to look after Butch pretty well, and maybe she could take some time off on weekends to ride her bike and keep their lawn down to a dignifiable level. She had decided early in the spring to let her past experiences at Camp Bustyerbritches over in Longview speak for themselves (and therein, for some sort of future reference, lies a tale or two). So she thought she had the time to do it, as far as that went.

But what if it all turned out to be a big batch of tickle tongue. What if it all went sour?

She for sure knew Mr. Charlie well enough to know he had high expectations for the joint. Try as she might, there was only so much she felt like she could do. And for what, really? Only half a promise of some future dough and half of an old man's crackers and sardines probably. Maybe one of the Boogers, or Frodo with his big insulated feet, would be a better choice. Maybe she wasn't the one.

But, as you can imagine, that line of inquiry didn't last for long. Just for about half a whirl in the puny wind, but no longer. She was the one. No one else willing to work for nowhere near minimum wage was as experienced in the field of ponditude as she was. No one else knew the lay of the land. She hadn't even shown Mr. Charlie where the treasure was buried yet. It wasn't much of a treasure, just some plastic jewelry her folks had gotten on a church retreat to Las Vegas (don't even ask) sealed up in a bag and a sort of a time capsule filled with some below average book reports they were supposed to sign for; Allie was gonna let those ferment for another five years. But still, she was the one.

She pulled at the last of the mess lodged in her teeth. "Okay," she said.

That was enough for Mr. Charlie. His work there was done; even though they had only hardly started, that was good enough for the day. He unleashed the rope, lowered her on down and took the knot out. Allie got her way out of the bag and stood there with sopping hair looking out at the ponds.

"Okay?" Mr. Charlie asked.

"Yeah. Okay," Allie burbled. "But just one thing."

She walked over to where the hose lay still gurgling. She clamped her thumb over the end and turned it in the direction of Mr. Charlie. Then she gave him a plum snooterful.

She soaked Mr. Charlie from his baseball cap to his boots with nothing like a laugh going on. This was serious. Being a girl, and you know a lot of what that's like no matter which side of the fence you're on, she figured she had one last chance, one last good chance, to set the foul poles. There were times when she would listen to Mr. Charlie, and there were times when he would have to listen to her. It was his house, and his big idea, and maybe even his lunch, but he would have to listen, too. Again, a lot of stuff to squirt through a hose, but it seemed to have the desired effect.

When she was finished, Mr. Charlie stood there with a dripping chin and a dripping everything and got kind of humbled for a moment. He looked at Allie and opened his yap like he was gonna speak. Then he considered the outrageousness of the situation, from one end of it to the other, and he just about broke down laughing. Allie humphed a little, then she walked back by the shed and turned off the hose. She came back and stood by Mr. Charlie while he dumped water out of his boots. He turned and went into the house, brought out two worn out swim towels and carried them to the picnic table. They dried off their clothes and mopped out their ears for a while. Mr. Charlie sat down on the table next to her, considering all that he and this wilted little ragamuffin had already done and all that lay still in store. "Okay, partner," he finally said. "Okay."

17.

A fiery geyser blew up at Bernice's end. Better put that another way. Out at the end of Bernice, where stood the hideous little house and the ponds as best they had done, Allie was setting bottle rockets off in the road. They were being doled out by Mr. Charlie from a laundry bag. He had collected fireworks off and on over the past few years, moving them from place to place and keeping them out of most moisturey situations until he had a good supply. He was much more measured about forking them over than Allie would have wanted. She kept scrambling up and holding out her hands like she was running low on porridge, but Mr. Charlie just counted out enough to fill the bottles again and then watched as she went among them lighting the fuses. They took off in formation into the dusky air and then shot in all different directions. Quite a few made it to the ponds, where they made a little poink under the water. Skee, the eternal watchdog for alien invasions, paddled after them and ate all the sticks. Without their guidance systems, he knew there'd be no hope of them reporting back to their home planet.

The guests began to arrive. There was nothing on the television but summer reruns, so most of them had been out playing chase or riding their bikes. It was still a ways to July the Fourth, so Allie and Mr. Charlie's display stuck out like a noisy inviting thumb. Each one got a sparkler or two from Mr. Charlie's judicious bag. Towards the last of the invitation he handed over some of his big guns, some actual skyrockets costing upwards of fifty cents. Allie shored up the bottles, got some other kids and arranged for them to be blasted off in a finale on the count of three. One of them burst apart right on the spot, but the rest hit the mark, blistering the night and announcing, for good and all, that something big was happening over at the old Ambolini place.

The kids walked into the yard and stood around the picnic table. They had laid out a bunch of popcorn, a pan of brownies Allie's mom had fixed and some canned clams Mr. Charlie had found under the sink. There was also a washtub full of non-brand name sodas. Some of the Boogers even showed up, riding over in one of their dad's station wagons. They stood in a little group over by Mr. Charlie's blaring radio, punting each other around and arguing over which song to listen to.

Now that there was some steadier light on the subject, Allie and Mr. Charlie went in the house and got on their pond warming garb. It wasn't much. Allie came out in her dad's diving mask and a cape made out of a highway trash bag. She tripped over the end of the bag, adjusted the mask to where she could see a little and sat down triumphantly at the foot of the steps leading back into the house. Mr. Charlie took up the top step, resplendified in a waiter's coat, some x-ray glasses and a witch's hat he had got from rooting around in the closet. It was Mrs. Ambolini's. She put it on every Halloween and stood by the front door over a black pot of dry ice, handing out candy and being unaware of the future fables.

It went on that way for about an hour. There were no speeches and no formalities (which figures). A few of the smaller kids set up a game of tag around the ponds, using a cherubic hiney as home base. Mr. Charlie stretched out on the steps and sang along to bits of whatever flashed by on the radio. Butch and his mom stopped in to gather up the brownie pan; not much of a reason, but the lizards had put on a command performance that evening, shouting "break a leg, break a leg," and bombarding the kitchen with Milk Duds. So she needed some air, too. Butch was presented with the last of the sparklers and hobbled around with them in the dark part of the yard, making flying saucer sounds and antagonizing Skee the Secret Agent.

It started to get late. Allie's mom rounded up some of the party guests, the ones who had just took out running when they heard all the commotion, crammed them into her car and gave them lifts home. The others brangled their bikes out of the fence and rode off, setting up the next day's activities among themselves. The Boogers aloofed their way back to the station wagon and drove off for last call at the Dairy Dive. Then there was no one new. Mr. Charlie switched off the radio and let it get quiet. The crickets picked up their cadence.

Once again, there was not a lot to be said. He dumped all the ice from the washtub and took the few remaining cans inside. Allie tossed the popcorn crunchies out for the raccoons. Mr. Charlie came back, rearranged his hat from where he had banged it atop the door frame and put his hand on Allie's shoulder. He pointed up at the sign. It wasn't much either. Allie had begged some butcher paper from the meat department at the grocery store and scrawled on it with a fat red marker. It hung down in front of the house. "Open For Bizness," it said.

So they were open. After days of digging around in the dirt, gathering up outdoor antiques and gagging on coffee, they were open. The only deal was a thing; something that Allie had picked up on. You probably have too. As far as you could see across the ponds and through the steamy Texas night, there wasn't a goldfish to be found.

18.

Allie took half a day off. She fiddled around in the garage for a little, smooshing some new handle grips with long plastic streamers onto Fnorrt and greasing up the chain. She watched a stock car race with her dad for a while, had some lunch with him and left.

You see a lot of smoke in Texas. It sticks out against the sky, and sometimes it signals bad juju. Those are usually the weekday smokes. Things still caught on fire around Bernice; the volunteers would drop whatever they were doing and gather at the fire station, trying to remember who had the keys for a minute and then ripping off for the fight. But on weekends it usually meant someone was burning brush or putting on a charity pig roast.

Mr. Charlie had no pig, which on top of everything else was a good thing. But he had a whole bunch of the other piled up at the edge of the driveway. As Allie came up she saw it crackling away. He moved around it with a rusty rake, overmessing with it like most men do. He repiled some of it, splatted at the stray flames with the well water and sang him some rhythm and blues. When he saw Allie walk up he aimed the hose at her, but then decided he'd better not. Skee was already there of course; when he saw the smoke he had suspected some sort of alien uprising, abandoned the rancid roadkill he was munching on and torn out to save everybody.

Allie thought Mr. Charlie had it under control, so she walked in the house and looked around. There on the table, weighed down by a couple of trashed sparkplugs and some banana bread from one of the actual original ladies' daughters, sat the catalogs. The goldfish catalogs. They were just some vague descriptions with a bunch of codes and prices, but there they were. Allie finned through them for a while, trying to remember a fish name or two to strut in front of Mr. Charlie, then she went back out to where he was working.

"When are they going to get here?"

"Monday. Tuesday. Something. I made all the calls this morning."

"But you don't have a phone."

"I took some change over to the pay phone early and made them. Some of them were closed on Saturday, but one wasn't."

"Did you get any comets?"

"Yeah. They're supposed to be big sellers. I got lots of them and some others. Plus some food and some stuff to put in the water. Makes 'em grow better."

"How long will you let them grow?"

"Long as it takes. Three or four weeks I guess. Then they'll be ripe for the selling. Then we get some more."

"How do we do that?"

"We just call up the same guy and place an order. I oughta have a phone by then."

"The selling part I mean."

"Well, I also bought a couple of swooshy nets. We gather up what we need and stick 'em in plastic bags. Then we add some air and away they go."

"You sure must know a lot about goldfish."

Mr. Charlie set down the hose. He thought hard for a second over the ponds.

"I wouldn't know nothing about goldfish. Not if they all got together and bit me in the behind."

19.

The Official Library Of Bernice (that was what the sign out front said, which gives you some info about what all went into it) was open for half a day on Sundays. In the morning Allie enticed the lizards a little, moving Butch's cereal bowl around while he whined, and then said goodbye. She waited at the front of the library while they vaulted open the doors and then skiffed her way inside. She went over to the Reference Section, which was mostly some outdated car manuals dropped off by the latest generation of McKees, and scrumbled around looking for goldfish books. She found a couple of fat ones on tropical fish overall, but from what she knew tropical involved pineapples and hammocks. That was not what this was gonna be. She set them aside in case. The Kid Section (again, what the sign read) just had books about talking goldfish and such; you've read some of those. Then, over in the Adult Arena (a misspelling which actually fit), she found what she was after. A green book which didn't look like it'd been handled a lot around there.

It said "Growing Goldfish: A Handbook for Breeders." Allie guffed a little at the title. She knew what she could about breeding from science class; she was pretty sure none of that was gonna be going on, not as unromantic as they had left it all beneath the surface. But the growing part caught her eye. She laid the book flat out on a table so none of the monitors would see the word "breeders" and think something funny was going on (give some applause where it's due; that coulda said fishy.) For the most of the afternoon she plowed through it, scribbling in what was left of one of Butch's red tablets from school. She took a break and spun through a few children's books about farming for full exposure, but mostly she scribbled. A couple of her friends stopped over from the science fiction section to ask if she wanted to go for ice cream, but she whooshed them away. Time was tight, and there was only so much she could do.

Monday morning she ran up to Mr. Charlie. "They're eurythermal!" she yelled. Mr. Charlie spun around and looked behind him, expecting to see a bunch of outer space paratroopers falling from the sky. But all he saw were some turkey buzzards gliding around over the creek looking for a meal.

"What, the buzzards?"

Allie smacked herself on the forehead. "No. Goldfish. That means they can adjust themselves to put up with the heat." She flipped open the tablet. "And they have hundreds of varieties and two sets of fins. And no scales on their heads."

She followed Mr. Charlie around the yard, into the shed a couple of times and even over to the creek. She filled his brain with all kinds of gibberish about goldfish, how they came from China and were related to carp and weren't all that good for eating (unless you were joining a fraternity, her dad had said, when she had practiced in the living room the night before). When she was done she snapped her library work shut and looked at him. Mr. Charlie gave a distracted "hmmm" to all she had to offer.

He was looking at the road. A blue panel van was approaching. It went on by, stopped for a moment and approached again from the other side. The driver got out and had a grimaced look at the ponds. He backed the van in, barely missing the little one, went on around and opened it up.

There were big plastic tubs full of little plastic bags. All the goldfish were inside those, rippling at the top of the water. Allie crawled in and they set up a bucket brigade. The driver got the bags from her and gave them to Mr. Charlie, who identified them pretty good and put them in the different ponds to get adjusted. He set himself up an identifiable whistle from a film about the war while he worked.

Then he stopped midwhistle. The guy was walking over with a big mistake. A big varietal mistake in a bigger plastic bag. It was pretty hard to hold on to; he rolled it over and over in his hands. Allie, who had just been yanking out bags and setting them on the lip of the van without identifying anything, walked up and had a look. From all her book learning she knew what it was. It was a celestial, a gorgeous gold celestial. It had flabbery gelatinous eyes and it looked up at you like the last thousand years of Chinese history was all wrapped up in them. It was also pretty expensive, but the driver checked and it was nowhere on the bill. He didn't want to have to go back with it and get bawled out, so he just held out the stowaway and looked at the two of them hopefully. "We'll take it," said Mr. Charlie.

They finished with the rest and got the supplies out. They paid cash money for the unmistaken fish and all of it. The guy left them a receipt and a business card and drove away. Mr. Charlie carried the celestial over to the baby pool. He put it in all by itself.

This one fish, this only one for however long it all lasted, was to be off limits to any buyers of any things aquatic. He wanted to drive that point home, so Allie climbed into his moldy car with him and gave out directions across town to Nelligan's Fart and Raunch Supply (her name for it, naturally), where they got a little chicken wire and some stakes. Allie hammered the stakes in by the pool and wrapped the wire all around while Mr. Charlie put the goldfish vitamins into the other ponds – he guessed the big one didn't need them – and unleashed the onslaught. Goldfish came swirling out of the bags, glimmering around in the bubbles for a moment and then heading off to find out what in the heck they'd been poured into. Mr. Charlie came walking over to the driveway. Allie was pounding a sign into the ground in front of the chicken wire, a stinky little sign on a stinky little stick, but one that said it all: "Goliath. The Goldfish. Keep Out."

20

Buhrrang is a pretty good word. It was probably once made out of nothing, like most of this, but it's useful in lots of cases. It's the sound of someone dropping pans on the kitchen floor the split second before they start screaming. It's the sound of two trash cans being knocked together as you bring them in off the street at night. It's the sound of a lot of stuff. And, in Bernice, on this one day, it was the sound of something else.

Allie's mom had dropped her off in front of Mr. Charlie's in their pickup. She wanted to audition some green grassy carpet for the patio from a place over in Atlanta (there's a Texas one) that was having a sale, so she and Allie's dad had traded cars. Her mom knew how to drive a stick shift alright; when she herself was a kid, Allie's grandfather on her side had jerked along with her on some back roads, which the vast majority of them were, until she could go from gear to gear without being pitched onto the floorboard.

Allie pulled her bike out of the bed and set it down near Goliath. He was puddling around in his new home, looking up at the sky and contemplating his future as best he could fathom. Allie strolled into the house and poured herself some water. Then, from back behind the shed, she heard the word. Buhrrang. And again, Buhrrang.

She ran on out. Mr. Charlie was back there with a disheveled pipe wrench. He was using it in a most non-constructive appearing way, whacking the turn of the big pipe from the well and looking about as determined as could be. Allie stood way back and watched.

Mr. Charlie whacked and buhrranged and seemed to make an utter fool of himself for about another three minutes. Then he stopped, gasped a little and dropped the wrench on the ground. He twisted around and started to stumble away. That's when he saw Allie.

Even after half a day spent, and apparently mostly wasted, in the library, she could think of only one thing to say. "Well?"

Mr. Charlie smiled. This was a more serious and somehow more knowing smile. "Well, sweetie," he said, "Yesterday was Memorial Day. In all the ruckus I just forgot. But it's still a special day to me. Always will be."

Allie knew about Memorial Day. Even though vacation usually kicked in just before then, her teachers always gave them a few lessons, showed them some newsreels and then had them make paper flags and stick them out on the front lawn before they all got away for the summer. A lot of them still stood there.

"When I was off in the war there wasn't much to do. There was no way to really express yourself, and if you did it just got you doing the dishes in the galley. I spent most of my free time in my bunk, reading old letters and thinking about home. You'd get jolted awake by the sound of our guns as airplanes attacked us, waiting for the guns to get bigger as they got closer and for the alarms to sound. That meant you had to run. I hope you never have to know what that's like. Which I guess is one of the reasons I did it all in the first place."

Allie had to gulp a little. It was just one word that had got Mr. Charlie going, but she let him go. "Then late one summer I was down in the engine room doing my job. Most of the time I ran the desalinator so we had something to drink. The only guys who could do it down there in the heat were me and a kid from Louisiana. We drank the warm water and ate salt pills until the salt was running out our backs." Allie swallowed hard.

"I was trying to convince a machine to get going again with a ball peen hammer. Then all of a sudden the speaker they had hanging in there squawked up. One of the old chiefs told us we were done. The other guys had been talked, and more, into the terms of what they called the Potsdam Conference. Didn't have much to do with me, but it did mean was I was going back home."

"I gripped that hammer up and went over to the biggest of the pipes I could find. I didn't even care what might be in it. I banged on it to beat the band. An officer, guys we didn't see much of, came down in a hula skirt and looked all lieutenanty at me like that was gonna change things. It didn't. That day, on and off until the end of my shift, it seemed to me I made more noise than anyone in the Pacific Ocean. Then I went back to bed and waited to get in trouble." Mr. Charlie put on a prideful smile and jabbed Allie in the ribs. "Somehow I never did."

"Now, no matter where I am, I guess no matter when, no matter what I got to work with, I do that all again. I do it for all the wars and for all my friends, the ones who didn't make it and the ones that did. I do it for all the ones I didn't know. And I do it for you and your little brother."

Mr. Charlie walked over and took up the wrench. He whaled it on the pipe one more time. Buhrrang. Then he just walked off. Allie gathered up some goldfish food and threw it around in the water. She thought maybe Mr. Charlie had other stuff to do in his head, and that maybe they were done for the day.

But, as often happened, they weren't exactly. Mr. Charlie had set himself up halfway across the yard. From there, facing away at the creek, he was leading a universal chorus of a universal song, jabbing his arms out and around like a street crusader. Allie moved in a bit, listened long enough and then backed away. She climbed on Fnorrt and rode home, singing some of Mr. Charlie's song as she went:

Oh, the sun may shine through the London fog
Or the river run quite clear,
Or the ocean brine turn into wine
Or I forget my beer
Or I forget my beer me boys
Or the landlord's quarter pay
But I'll never forget my own true love
Ten thousand miles away.

21.

The next morning a bunch of Bernicians (they had actually voted on that one), some retired guys in cowboy hats, came over and took a look. The thing about communists, which had put them off for a while, had all blown over. A college kid with a summer job at the county had heard the initial gossip as it wildfired its way through town. He thought he could use Mr. Charlie and his social struggle as the subject of an overdue anthropology paper, so he pulled up one day and followed him around, working the word "Comrade" into his sentences like a nervous disciple. Mr. Charlie just looked at him unknowingly, said "Bubba" back and went on his way. The kid had told everyone that if the struggle going on at that improbable plantation was what communism was all about, they really didn't have any worries.

The guys did their own kind of cowboy toodling around the grounds, advising Mr. Charlie on where he had taken wrong turns and how to sturdy it all up. Sturdying was an activity that somehow had never even occurred to Mr. Charlie, but he drifted among them saying "uh huh" and getting hungry. After they galloped away in their gallant old pickups, he got out some raspberry yogurt and some tuna fish and mixed it all in together. Mr. Charlie was not a plain fellow at all; he preferred vanilla yogurt with his tuna, but the grocery store had been out so he had to make do. Do. Allie reported in and he offered her some out of the bowl, but she just looked in it and felt something churdling in her throat.

Mr. Charlie washed out the bowl. They went on out and got to it. The sturdy suggestions still hadn't really caught hold with him, but some weeds were coming up around the rocks and so they pulled and snipped while Allie taught him the current hits off the Saturday radio. She got up to the biggest of them, and then she remembered something, and then she quit.

"What was that all about yesterday?"

Mr. Charlie thought he had explained it all pretty well. "A tribute. Just some sort of a tribute."

"No, I know that part. But the song."

He kept his focus on some young dandelions. His own dad had stood over him whenever he went to their house to trim it all up, watching as he pulled at the weeds and sipping on iced tea. When he got to dandelions, Fatherkins always offered the same annual advice, in what seemed to Mr. Charlie to be a critiquey sort of way: "Their roots run really deep." Now, he had a nagging respect for dandelions. Their roots ran really deep.

"Well," he said, "we had a few soldiers on board the ship for the bad times. One of them had been on other boats and learned some sea chanties. We sang them at chow sometimes. That was one of 'em."

"But not even that." Allie lowered the snippers and looked him over. "Did you ever love a girl?"

He thought a bit. "Nope," he said. "Well, I loved my mom and most of my cousins that were girls. But no."

"Really no?"

Mr. Charlie lost his focus. He swapped at the dandelions and let them lay. "Well," he said, "yeah."

"We left the empty ocean and sailed for Japan. They dressed us all up in Tokyo Bay and had us stand on the deck while both side's brass signed the surrender on another ship. Then we went to China and drove around on some rivers. Finally, we went to Hawaii, to start to be finally done."

"I tried to go surfing there. A guy rented me a board at Waikiki Beach and gave me some Vaseline to rub all over me, which was all he had to give. I had been down there in that engine room, and not much of any place else, for so long I looked like a paper cup. I thought maybe the Vaseline would help in the sun. I paddled out sitting on that thing and when I hit the waves good I laid down for my first ride."

"Not much of a ride. All that Vaseline mixed in, or didn't, with the wax and latched on to nothing. I slid off the end of her like a seal and sputtered around in the water for a minute. I was out beyond all the waves. I swam down the board and climbed on real careful. My surfing days were done, but I thought maybe I could just take a nap."

"One thing they didn't teach us in survival swimming was that water moves both ways. I woke up a while later and looked around. All I could see of all of Hawaii was Diamond Head and a little of the Pacific Princess Hotel. I was back out in the ocean. I started working my way back, using just the tips of my fingers and the pink tower on the hotel for a guide. Finally some fishermen from the air base came by and gave me what amounted to a lift. They tossed out a rope and floated out some beers. I could tell over the motor they were having a pretty good time with it. I made it back across the waves, turned the surfboard in fast as I could and went straight back to my bunk. One of the guys gave me a couple of his flowery necklaces, but that was all there was to Hawaii."

It was a good little story. A good little spinout. But Allie knew Mr. Charlie had been using it to avoid something. She stabbed the snippers into the ground. "What does that have to do with girls?"

Mr. Charlie sniffed a little through his nose and gnawed on his thumb. "Alright," he said.

"We left Pearl Harbor and went on to San Diego. That was where they were gonna cut us loose. Most of the others ran downtown in their show uniforms to get kissed. I think they had some fun. Me, I just went over to the train station with the papers they gave us and tried to match them up with a ride to Texarkana. It seemed to be not the most popular of destinations, so for a couple days I hung around the lunch counter. They had what they called an Uncle Sam Special, some glowing hammy stuff and what all swimming around in this indescribable gravy for a dime or two. I ate a lot of those."

"She was." Mr. Charlie swallowed hard as could be. "She was in there waitressing. She had pretty eyes. Eyes like shattered marbles, and a kind of a big nose. I was always a sucker for those. She moved around that counter patting sailors on the hands and pouring coffee. She sang Broadway numbers and handed out platters of gruel like there was no tomorrow. And she smiled through it all. Her smile was something you could sink your teeth into. She always had on a pink uniform that made her swish when she walked and some clunky white shoes. To me she was dressed for the ball."

"I talked to her as much as I could. She had family all around there. Her dad was a truck driver for a fish house and her mom kept the books. She had hopes of going to college up in Berkeley and being a dance teacher or something. I made up a few lies about my future and what it was gonna be. She didn't even try to see through them; she just patted my wrist and said it was all great. Then she would walk away to tend to the others sitting there. But it seemed like she was always looking back at me. I finally figured out I was sitting by the time clock, but I could still think that."

"I hung out in there most of whenever she was working. An old soldier from the first big war talked to me a little, trying to get me to take in the sights, but I just sat there drinking coffee and watching her walk around. I even asked her to go with me to the movies, thinking I could borrow the money somehow, but she said she was busy.

Maybe tomorrow night she said. Tomorrow night didn't come for us. They had generated enough interest in Texas to put a train together, so I got my separation all done the next day and got on board."

Some kids came in the front gate, the very first ones looking for goldfish. Should have been a big occasion, at least deserving of a smoke bomb or two, but Allie told them they were taking a union break – she'd heard of those from her Dad – and to come back later. Mr. Charlie didn't even notice. He went on.

"I rode it all the way to Texarkana. I got off in the middle of a winter's night. My folks had sent me a letter saying that Daddy had taken a job in the oil fields in Arkansas and they were moving. The town was called Fouke. Still don't know why it would be called something like that. But there's monsters there, in the swamps and all. I reread the address and started walking."

"An old yellow taxi picked up my trail out across the viaduct. The driver kept circling around in the dark, trying to get me to take a ride, but like always I didn't have nothing. Finally he just took me for that. I bumped open the door to the new house and Momma came boiling out of their bedroom in her night gown. She cried and hugged me up for a good long while. I was done with it."

Mr. Charlie was spinning out again. Then he brought it all back. "But I never got her off my mind, that waitress. I've had dates with plenty of women and done a lot of stuff to try to make it happen, a lot of outlandish stuff, but nothing works. I still see her on the street sometimes, with her hair all done up in the back, but it's never really her. Never has been."

Allie noodled at the top of the snippers. "You should have said something to her."

"Yeah. Something. I sent a letter with some more lies in it to the train station with her name on it, what I had off her uniform at least, but it came back unopened. I guess she was gone from there."

The kids had figured break time must be up, so they walked back into the yard. Allie glanced at Mr. Charlie, then she got up off the ground and wiped her hands on her pants. She started to head on over and then she looked back at him.

"What was her name?"

Mr. Charlie sniffed a little bit more and gazed at the dandelions. "Rebecca. Miss Rebecca," he said. "That's all I ever had."

22.

The selling turned out to be the easy part; at least there was one. Kids from all over suddenly had a thirst for goldfish and their bawdy bowls. The dime store in town ran out of the bowls lickety split; they never had had any fish to sell, so for years they just sat there collecting cobwebs. Four or five kids and one or two moms a day would drive to the TG & Ys over in the next towns and clean them out too. They'd get them set up with lots of candy colored rocks and some water, then show up at the ponds to populate them. By that time, though, the shoppers were a little low on funds. Mr. Charlie set up a sliding price range without Allie's approval, which made for a pretty bad bottom line. After a while he started putting together a bag with one or two fish and just keeping his mouth shut. Kids started pulling stuff out of their pants you wouldn't believe. It went around that the price of one goldfish was nine pecans. Or two army men and a rubber band. One little girl Allie hardly knew got one for a lock of cat hair out of her purse.

That just wasn't gonna work. Allie's mom made them a pie out of the pecans, and Skee kept some spitty soldiers swaddled up in his cheeks in case of a final rocket insurrection, but it just wasn't gonna work. Mr. Charlie's worst suit of all, it seemed, was a sense of business. Allie found what he thought were his records one day. They were sitting there on the back of the toilet. He had put some columns in a notebook:

Fish In   Fish Out   Money

He made daily entries there on the throne, scribbling with a stub of a pencil and being otherwise occupied with some other stuff. The columns were pretty crappy. Lots of fish were coming in, and about the same amount were going out, but the money part was swirling right down the hole. They had to do something.

Allie got to thinking. Whenever she rode with her dad to gas up one of their vehicles, whenever she paid attention at checkout lines, just about whenever whatever, the adults in charge would kinda cuss about these people. The people called the middle men. The ones who would stand in the way, holding up all that was holy about all there was to business in Bernice, collecting their cuts and driving around in nice cars. All the money was in the middle. From what she could make of it, being a middle man was about the most dastardly thing you could do.

So, natural as could be, they became middle men.

It took her another day to bring Mr. Charlie up to speed. Then he stuck some advertising in a couple of classifieds in the backs of fish magazines. He pulled on one of his two ties, the one without the dancing girls, and loped over to some Woolworth's and all in his car handing out price lists for bags of fish. The store managers had heard about the goings on in Bernice. By then, the kids had even put on a Goldfish Parade through town, lugging their bowls along in wagons and giving away prizes. The Grand Prize was a ride home on the back of a septic tank truck, but a picture of it all had made the local paper. That perked up the store's ears to where they arranged for some other eager middle men to head on out to Mr. Charlie's. He still had to chase a few down and convince them they had found the right place, but it started to work. He and Allie bagged up enough fish to fill the orders and then got some more, trying to avoid the worst of the middle men. One tried to sell them some siding for the house. Mr. Charlie just tossed all the money into the box – they were on a cash and carry basis - and, with Allie's help, counted it out at the end of each day. Then he tossed it back in.

The notebook got clogged with cash. Finally they went to the bank and opened up an actual account. It was called "Operating Fund/A & C, LLC." They had no clue what an LLC was, never would, but it sounded good to the lady who made it up behind the counter. And so did the money; they fisted all the bills over and counted out the coins. She didn't know what she could really do with the last of the pecans, but she set them in the paper clip bowl with a smile. Mr. Charlie and Allie went out and celebrated with cherry Icees. They carried them back to the ponds, handed out some more fish and looked after the rest for the day, slinging around their supplements and inspecting for the dreaded diseases Allie had read about.

Look, you're not really gonna learn much about raising goldfish from this. Maybe about keeping them hydrated and fed a little, but not much else of nothing. Maybe all of this amounts to mostly a metaphor; might behoove you to look that one up. But do be careful with those. You're gonna be told to read a lot of books in school, some real ones, with lights across the water and all kinds of emotions and other items. Your teachers will want you to watch for the metaphors. You can work them into class discussions unannounced and make them proud as punch. You can say this is a metaphor for that and all, which will stand you in good stead until you show up on Science Day with a plastic box of unattached wires and switches and say it's a metaphor for getting off the couch and actually doing something satisfactory. That just won't work, so be careful.

But, metaphorically speaking as they say, it all did satisfactory for a Texas summer. Goldfish came and went. They got lots of new bags and lots of new money. A banker from another town even came by and offered them something called a line of credit, doing his best to get in the middle of it all too, but Mr. Charlie just made him some gross coffee and then went on his way again. So, anyway, it all worked; let's leave that part alone for a while. We have some other fish to fry.

23.

One of them rose to the surface just as Allie was getting there. It was on the morning of a big windy day. She saw Mr. Charlie carrying a bunch of goldfish bags across the yard to a guy's car. He was being cautious in the wind, holding them with both hands, which meant he didn't have a way to hold on to his ball cap. A gust came up and knocked it off. It rolled up against Goliath's cage.

There was something Allie had never seen. It's gonna seem a little farfetched, but go back a bit and try to find something that isn't. She had never seen the top of Mr. Charlie's head. He always wore a hat or a cap or, one time in the kitchen when he heard Allie coming in, a saucepan. That was the one thing he seemed religious about, and there was a reason.

Up there was really something. He had not much hair all over overall, just some yellow and white stubble, which made the something even more so. He had a bunch of oversize seed beads holding together a bunch of long hair that now hung way down in his eyes. He kept walking and blowing at it and whipping it around, kind of annoyed at all the exposure. He got up to the guy and threw his head back, trying to pretend like nothing was happening. But, of course, something was; Allie was peeling to pieces in the yard.

She didn't know whether to act embarrassed for the old guy, but one glance around the place took care of that anyway. So she just wandered around like a befuddled spider, keeping a little distance and a little transfixed. Mr. Charlie did his deal with the guy, chunked the money in the box and unstuck his cap from the chicken wire. He laid his hair back on top of his head, put on the cap and walked away like he could rewind the last few minutes. No way, as you know, was Allie gonna let that happen.

She didn't have to not let it happen. Mr. Charlie walked back and cut in on the conversation that was going on in her cranium. "See," he said as was usual, "I was barely nineteen when I enlisted. I went away on the first of lots of trains to get it done. They didn't have much of a welcome mat laid out for us. I got off a bus from the station one morning and started getting yelled at. That happened a lot. They lined us up for shoes and uniforms and shots. No one knew where we were going, so we got lots of different shots. At some point," he said, "we got haircuts."

"I had been as fashionable a guy as I could be. I never had much to wear, but I wore it pretty well. I sold papers called Grit for money and spent it all on saddle shoes. Didn't go too well with coveralls, and it got me a funny reputation, but I didn't care. I did care about my hair though. I had a duck tail in the back and a puffy little pompadour up front. When I sat down in the barber's chair that day, I grabbed the front of it and I told the guy. I said he wasn't getting it."

"That caused a stir. A drill sergeant with a little soul came over and grumped at me a second. I guess I coulda started all my getting in trouble right there, but he told me just to move my hand back so my cap could cover it. The barber took about his standard ten seconds to do the rest of me up. There it was. I had almost a handful of hair to get me through. It said to me that, however it all turned out, I was my own different dodo of a person. I didn't belong to them. I still loved some people, but I didn't."

"I keep the rest of it pretty short. Mother Nature has had a hand in that over time. But other than tying it up like you can tell, and trimming up some of the fuzz, it's been that way ever since. I came close a few times, but I don't belong."

The spinning was settled. Mr. Charlie got some bags and started filling them with goldfish again, getting ready for the middling of the morning. Allie followed him around, still thinking all befuddled and staring at his cap. Then she hit on it. She jumped on Fnorrt and just took off.

Her mom was in the kitchen working on a crossword and monitoring something in the oven that smelled pretty good. There wasn't much else going on. So she asked her for a ride, and a little money, and quite a bit of understanding. When they got to Mr. Teddy's Barber Shop of Style, she swung her way up into the chair and told him to take it all off.

Mr. Teddy looked over at her mom. She just gave him a summery shrug and let him get to it. All of Allie's fine brown hair fell into belimbered piles on the checkerboard floor. Then, when he got to a spot, she grabbed it good and told him, too. "You ain't getting it." She looked over at her mom, who had arched her Eyebrow of Correction and aimed it right at her. Allie said, "You aren't getting it."

He worked his way around what she wasn't hiding and finished up. He put some bay rum on it all. They paid Mr. Teddy and walked out with Allie holding her hair up in her hands. Back home she wrapped it in rubber bands. She took a look in the mirror and put on a purple Boogers cap. Then she took off again.

Back at the place, Mr. Charlie was just pluddering around at the picnic table. Allie ran up and positioned herself real good in front of him. Then she took off the cap. Tahdah.

He stammered a bit. All the surprise in his face was actually tinctured with some anger, which was another thing Allie had never seen. Mr. Charlie loaded up a lot of it, the anger, and then he let some of it unload. "What did you do?"

Allie thought it was fairly obvious. For a second she tried to snap him out of it, flicking it like a stunted bullwhip and trying to get him to play along. Shoot, it was just for the summer. Her neck felt cooler and all the lack of brushing meant she'd get to work a little earlier. She didn't see the big deal.

But Mr. Charlie seemed to be taking it differently. She sat down beside him and said something about a lot of it all. "I just wanted to be like you."

Mr. Charlie leaned back and pulled on an eyebrow. Like him. There were times when that wasn't all that great. Like him could be lonely, and even when it wasn't it could be confusing. Like him was lying awake at night, thinking about the past and the future and wondering if hoot owls had a taste for goldfish. Like him was not being invited to go dancing, and always thinking about the one girl he had wanted most to twirl around. Like him was a lot of things, and some of them were things she shouldn't know a lot about.

But then, like him was also an adventure. He had to work at it, but it was. He had caught a good hammerhead in Florida, eaten lots of gumbo down around there and seen the northern lights all those years ago out on the ocean. He had done the watusi around a maypole in Atlanta. He was alone on that one, too, but it had made everyone laugh and that had made it worth it. And he had met a little girl, which was turning out to be the biggest adventure of all. A girl who, for no reason really unassailable, had admiration in her hazel eyes. He felt like some degree of disappointment was in store for her, as it always seems it has to be, but it wasn't gonna be on whatever there was of his watch. He turned to her a little and knuckled her on the head. "I like it, Allie," he said. "I like what you did."

24.

A pair of pony heads sat at Allie's kitchen table. Mr. Charlie had been invited to dinner. The head coach for the Oilers, a guy Mr. Charlie admired, said you always take your hat off inside. Inside barely applied back home, but here he tossed it over his chair. In between bites of his meatloaf, Butch was fully flabbergasted. He kept reaching over with his unforkfilled hand, working Mr. Charlie's hair into somethings like shadow puppets and giggling. Finally he just put down his fork and stood up beside him. He took one half of what was available and faced it off against the other on a western Main Street. The dusty duelers approached each other, then a shot rang out. They must not have been very good at it, because it winged Butch, who grabbed his chest and fell on the floor.

Allie's mom came over from the oven. The biscuits had been slow to finish, but she set them down in front of Mr. Charlie next to a bowl of red-eye gravy. He didn't even bother with the butter; he opened a couple and poured the gravy all over them. He looked at them. "They had these in the jail," he said.

Butch became instantly healed. He stood up and inched a little away. Allie and her Dad looked at him real good while her Mom set the pot holders on the counter. Then she looked at him, too. Allie had a little follow up to what he had said. "You were in jail?"

"Well, honey," Mr. Charlie said, "Not like you think. I do know people who have really been there. Your folks probably do, too. Most of the time it don't amount to much. But it did to me."

"We did our shakedown cruise to Trinidad and then back to Boston. One day we got our real orders. We were going to the Pacific for the duration. We sailed back down the coast and took a turn for New Orleans. That was the last place in America we were gonna be. And I knew it might be for good."

"They let us off the ship for the last night. I messed around by myself. I had some coffee and dolled up donuts and just took it all in. Saw a lot of my shipmates weaving in and out of bars, but I kept to myself. I wanted pretty bad to avoid them for that one night. And I really wanted to avoid the ship. But I needed a place to sleep, so I wandered over to the police station and asked if they had any ideas. The desk clerk offered me a cell. Resembled the place I was supposed to be in for a long time, but I took it."

"The lights stayed on for it. I wrapped my head in a blanket and just lay there thinking. A guy a couple doors down kept yelling about the Cincinnati Reds. Guess he must've done something real. But when the sun came up they gave me some of these biscuits and gravy off the meal cart and sent me on my way. I took the last of my cash and bought a Singapore Sling at Pat O'Brien's. Seemed like the right drink at eight in the morning. There was a lady sitting next to me at the bar looking like she'd just fallen off a parade float. Said she always dressed that way. That was another thing I felt like I was fighting for. I finished my drink and walked on the ship. Then we just left on out."

Mr. Charlie looked around a bit. He did a mannery little nod to Allie's mom and dug right in.   The biscuits disappeared in a manner of moments, then he had two more with the leavings on his plate. Allie's mom smiled and squeezed her husband's knee under the table. There was some good Blue Bell ice cream for dessert; the folks over in Brenham had come up with some pretty cool concoctions. The lizards stopped by Butch's place and larooped a little of it on his chin and his nose and his pants. Then dinner was done.

They all walked into the living room. Allie's dad showed Mr. Charlie some deer horns mounted on lacquered boards and some macrame Allie had done for them at camp. They watched some boxing on the TV and then they all walked Mr. Charlie out to what there was of his car. He set his take home biscuits on the roof, raised the hood and hit the motor with the spotlight for a second, just to prove there was something workable under there. Butch got up on the front bumper, pulled off his cap and fixed a final rabbit out of his hair. Then Mr. Charlie shut the hood and said his goodbyes. Allie's family walked into the street, looking up at the stars. A plane from the big new DFW airport growled overhead on its way to New Orleans. Allie watched it for a while. Then she turned to her parents. "This was nice," she said.

25.

The morning, though, was not nice. It was just hot. The weather lady had gone out of her way to warn them about a heat wave, which seemed to Allie a little redundant. But it wasn't redundant at all, this one. It came waving up from the coast and whipped out a ton of itself. Allie stepped into the driveway early and felt it snatch onto her. From the kitchen window it had looked like a normal day, but that melted away fast. She got Fnorrt out of the garage and just started walking slow, pushing him along on the road.

The wave hadn't broken by the time it had reached Mr. Charlie's. The dandelions were all drooped over and the cherubs were hanging on by a wing and a prayer. Goliath was huddled under some toy trucks, some floaters, that Butch had dropped in there and pushed around with a mop handle to entertain him.

Mr. Charlie himself was kneeling down beside a pond. Looked like there might be some trouble. He kept reaching over in it and pulling something out. Some of the new fish. They hadn't adjusted themselves fast enough in this heat, and they hadn't made it. That had happened to a few before for all kinds of reasons, including the raccoons, but this was a catastrophe.

Allie walked up to him. There was a little gold pile there between his knees. Mr. Charlie pulled some more out and looked them over for signs of life. Then he let them slip between his fingers.

Nothing was said. She took the burnrake and swirled it around in the water, doing what she could to help. They got them all out and moved on to the next, and then the next. Three little piles of little goldfish finally lay beside the ponds. Mr. Charlie stood there looking hard at the fence. Allie reached up and, for only the second time, took his hand in hers. She said something. "Do you hate it when they die?"

Mr. Charlie looked even harder. Something in his mind, some big equation, wasn't working out. It was close, and it might still get solved over what was left of the summer, but it just wasn't. He sighed a little and let go of her hand. "Go home, Allie," he said. "Just go home."

She didn't at first. She forced herself onto Fnorrt for the roasted ride to the library, where she got the book out again and looked hard for something she'd missed. It just wasn't there though. It looked like they were on their own. She saw a copy of

"Seventeen," so she flipped through it a bit and read about all the new makeup she wasn't wearing. She was doing her best to do what she was told; she was just staying away.

Allie stayed away for the rest of the day. She found Billy and Frodo and slopped around with them on a Slip 'N Slide in Billy's back yard. His mom came out after a while and told them they were laying too much of a trench in the grass, so they had to stop. Frodo's feet weren't helping. But she had some decent chocolate chip cookies for them, and so they laid around on the covered patio catching up. Appeared Billy had a new girlfriend. Also appeared she didn't know about it; he rode over to the new apartments she had just moved into every afternoon on his bike, skulking around and trying to catch her outside playing. If he did, he just got up to the corner where she couldn't see him and gave out a Tarzan yell.

Then he would tear away. So she was a typical girlfriend.

After a while Allie headed home. She played what Butch called pacheezlee with him for a bit, then her folks rounded them up and took them for burgers at the Dive. Allie knew in advance it was gonna be a hard night. She kept wanting to head back over. She had stuck her night stick in the closet that one night, and she figured it would still be there. He was probably ticklish, too. Maybe that would get him going again. But he had said to stay away. She guessed that much, and not much more, was his right as the senior partner, but she still wanted to.

She was up at the first fingers of light. Not really though. She had tossed so much her covers had her good. Her legs were all mummified and her shoulder had gone to sleep. She looked over at her scissors, but that would be one she wouldn't get away with. So she oozed up to the head of the bed and launched herself out on the floor. She just put on her work clothes from yesterday. Her dad was gone, but her mom and her brother were still undignifying themselves. Butch was saying something in his sleep about Allie cheating at his game (which she had been, but in a sisterly sort of way).

The wave had petered out. It was still hot, but not so bad she couldn't ride. She went on in and walked around. Mr. Charlie wasn't there. She pushed open the bathroom door a little, looking for his knees to be perched there, but they weren't. He wasn't in the shed or over by the graves either. That guy could sure get away.

He came up from the creek in a wandery way. He'd been down there watching for something. His eyes were big and crazy; there was a look in them Allie knew about. Butch had an unhealthy fear of tardy slips, so lots of times he took off for school ahead of her. She had caught up with him on Fnorrt one morning while some new kids, the Carter twins, were introducing themselves. Their form of introduction involved knocking his books and his pencils out on the road and pushing him around. Allie's head had started pounding and her eyes got that same kind of crazy. She slammed her bike right into the middle of the receiving line and let them know just what was up. "That's my brother," she said. After all that, the twins became Butch's best big friends. Self-preservation mechanisms can be wonderful things.

Mr. Charlie, though, was acting like he was out of preserves. Allie looked at where he was heading and caught on. She'd been so distracted about disturbing him on this different day that she had snuck through the yard without seeing Goliath's cage had been destroyed.

It was Mr. Charlie that had done it. He had heard a bunch of splashing in the night and run out hatless in his pajamas. He pulled out the chicken wire and all the trucks and got down in the dark water. He threw Goliath in the nearest pond and then he got a hoe.

Allie looked over and saw half of what he'd been hoeing there on the ground. Wrapped up and around what there was of itself was part of a big snake. The other half was draped over the fence. She walked over to the fence, where its face was, and had a look. She could tell from the icky part of science it was a water moccasin. Those are bad.

"It tried to get him," said Mr. Charlie. "I knew it'd be back if I didn't do something definite. So I did what I did. I just couldn't let him get Goliath."

Allie felt a little wobbly. She fought down some sickly stuff riding up in her gullet. Then she wobbled over to Mr. Charlie and gave him a hero's hug. There weren't lots of those that summer; hawking goldfish doesn't really give rise to much in the way of heroics. But this time it was deserved. She laid her head on his belly and squeezed. That took away most of the crazy. He patted Allie on the back a couple of times and walked away. Then he picked up a shovel and went over to the corner by the creek.

Allie found Goliath hovering by one of the cherubs. He thought, after all the hysterics, he'd been given a new home. It wasn't bad; he had more room to grow and the breathability was about the same. But the other goldfish had different ideas. They knew it was rare that they ate each other, but if it was to happen, then this was the one who could get it done. He'd paddled over to play with what they were afraid was his food.

They mostly wanted nothing to do with him; a few of the appetizer sized young ones swam up and took a look into his jiggly eyes, then returned as fast as they could to the fold. So, for the next hour or so, he had just done battle by himself with a blue truck that had landed in there and waited to be re-rescued.

Allie netted him up and put him back in the pool. She put all the chicken wire in place and stuck in the sign. Then she had a look at Mr. Charlie, who was digging a hole. From where she was it looked a little too skinny to be good for much, but he got it done and walked over to the piece of snake by the driveway. He laid it across the shovel and added the headpiece from the fence. Then he walked over and laid it all in.

Allie walked up to him. She saw three rounder, and thus more reasonable, little holes covered up closer to the fence. She felt like this was some of the crazy kicking back in. Dead snakes were for the garbage, or mostly for leaving alone. But Mr. Charlie refilled the hole with the dirt and bopped it on down. He put his hands on top of the handle and sang what he could of "Blessed Assurance." Then he looked at her. "Yes, Allie," he said. "I hate it when they do. I hate it when anything has to."

26.

There's one thing you're never careful about. You're not really supposed to be, and that right there is part of the problem. The thing is that summer slips away. You can plan all kinds of stuff for it, especially at the beginning, but then the bike trails wherever you are look pretty good and most of your plans progress southward into loogeying off bridges and lying under oak trees. That stuff has merit, and you should fit it in as long you can. But it doesn't slow down summer.

Allie's family went to the beach for the second week of August. Grandma Betsy gave Allie some more shirts she had found out looking for sea shells. Some of them advertised the kinds of things that led the original owners to lose them; her Mom took control of those. Her dad caught some redfish on a jetty near the house, and Butch and Allie ran around on the sand at night with a big gray Radio Shack flashlight chasing fiddler crabs back into the gulf. Sometimes a tanker would honk its way past out in the big water, and Allie would watch it for a while. She missed the old man. She had asked Billy to look in on Skee and him, but she felt like Mr. Charlie needed it more. He needed her help.

When they got back in range of Bernice, Allie asked them to drop her off. Her Mom daubed a little aloe vera on her by the car and warned her that her laundry would still be waiting. From where she was it looked like he had handled it all okay; a delivery guy was putting some bags of new fish in the ponds. She hugged Mr. Charlie and then she perused the situation more fully. Still, nothing needed doing that she could see, so she walked over to where the fish were being paid for. This guy was new to all of it; even though Mr. Charlie was holding out a wad of bills like always, he thought maybe he needed some sort of identification. So, to get it over with, Mr. Charlie dug out his worn down wallet, another thing Allie had never seen, and pulled out his license.

The picture wasn't bad. Mr. Charlie had tucked his hair in behind his ear and tried not to look like he was on trial. But there was one thing that was. Allie had another look and backed up. The Boogers had their first game, a practice one against an even smaller town, in two Fridays. She knew what day of the month that was. That meant tomorrow was Mr. Charlie's birthday.

She lay all night on top of the covers. Butch got up and waggled his way into the living room once, looking for water. He wound up stuck behind a big chair in the dark and tuned up for a cry. Allie got off the bed at the first note and turned him around. She put him back in bed and got him a drink. Then she went back to planning.

Allie had a lot of credits built up in Bernice. Credits are an overall good thing. They come in handy when six weeks are almost up and your toes aren't at the line. And they come in handy when you have to throw the most magnificent surprise party there ever was, and all you have is a day. Allie and Fnorrt rode all over town cashing in credits. Some of them were for things she had done and some were for what she hadn't. She reminded the folks at the grocery store that she hadn't busted all the pumpkins that they had left by the back door for a whole afternoon last October. That was good for a case of fruit punch. She reminded the drug store people that she had, in fact, ridden some cough syrup over to McKee Auto Supply when they were all busy. That got her some crepe paper and a birthday card.

The lady at the dress shop had already given her mom some pajama patterns in return for Allie not letting Butch run the back half of a burrito through a sewing machine, but she let her sort buttons for a while to earn some bunting for the picnic bench.

Her mom drove in around noon and took it all home in her car. Allie laid it out in the garage. It looked like they were going picnicking on Pluto. There was a pound of beef jerky from the meat processing place, a bunch of balloons and a handful of bank calendars for door prizes. Allie had invited everyone she'd come in contact with, and told them to spread it around, so she knew there'd be a good crowd. The only thing left was a big one. She had to get Mr. Charlie gone. He had a habit of doing it on his own, but she couldn't depend on it. So, around three o'clock, she took Butch aside, explained it all to him and held out a couple of PayDays; one for now, one on completion.

A determined little boy with a half a tank of sugar rode his scooter toward Mr. Charlie's. The asphalt gave out about half way there, so he just threw it over his shoulder and started running. When he got there, Mr. Charlie was passing the hose over the ponds like a normal day. Butch handed him a note Allie had written:

"Mister Charlie,

Come quick. Butch's fish is sick.

Allie."

Mr. Charlie flipped it over. He didn't see much he could do, especially having ditched Allie's class the way he'd done. But he took out his pocket pencil and wrote on it.

"Be there soon."

Allie read the reply over Butch's huffing. She handed him the final PayDay and packed him in the car with all the party trappings. Her mom crept out of the driveway with her on the hood. She scanned the roads with her dad's old rifle scope, looking for Mr. Charlie and his corroded car. When she saw him she jumped in, rearranged Butch and his candy bar crumbs and told her mom to burn whatever rubber she was willing.

They took the nearest back way to the house and the ponds. Allie saw Mr. Charlie had left the hose on to fill the first one. She sent Butch around to turn it off and started unpacking. Her mom bunched up the bunting and put it all around with a stapler. Butch came back and started blowing up balloons. They tied them all over the fence and Goliath's chicken wire. Allie raked up the first of the leaves and all that was there in the yard; Skee, who had just shown up on his own, swallowed what wouldn't stick to the rake. A couple of guys from the meat shop came over with their sidewalk grill and set it up by the house. As soon as the smoke got rolling good, all the invitees took the signal and came driving over with faded green Tupperware bowls of potato salad and pickles and other good grub. Things were ready as they were gonna be. Now all Allie had to do was get Mr. Charlie back.

27.

The surprise part was still in play; the old guy barely even knew what was going on. He was standing in the back yard over at Allie's place, just waiting to be let in. He had spent some time figuring out Butch's rock polisher, and some more sweeping off the patio, but mostly he felt like an extra wheel for a while. When Butch finally came bursting into the yard he was standing there with his hands in his pockets, watching the sun start its way down. Allie had told her brother what to do; the most important part was not to say anything that would muck it up. So he ran up with his big eyes and a whimpery mouth and took Mr. Charlie by the wrist. He brought him into his bedroom and just pointed.

Trouble was, once again, there wasn't any trouble. Floobie the fish was toddering around in his bowl like normal, making the most of his day and waiting for dinner. Allie had thought about tossing in some ice cubes before they left to maybe slow him down a little, but by now it would've worn off anyway. Mr. Charlie got in close and looked him over. "Looks like he got better," he said.

He headed on out. Allie's mom was standing by his car with some soggy morning toast and jelly on a soggier paper plate. Mr. Charlie ate it while she tossed some baskets. She tried to get him into a game of horse, but he showed her his boots and got going.

He thought he heard his radio blaring between stations through his open windows as he came around the corner. But it was The Miserables just tuning up. Les the singer had the night watchman shift at the plant; whenever the band normally played, they rolled the dice and just let it sit for the evening. But he couldn't get off on such short notice, so the rest of the band was planning on playing some waltzes, and definitely "School's Out" while they still could.

Mr. Charlie slid up and stopped in the road. He got out with his car still running and just about fell over. Half the town, and then some, was standing in his yard singing "Happy Birthday." Some of the goldfish owners ran out and walked him in while Allie and a couple of the others touched off some snucken skyrockets from behind the house. An old farmer with the most experience running dangerous machines moved his car off the road and shut it down. Then, in the light from a lot of tiki torches and a couple of smudge pots, it was party time in Texas.

Some of the cowboys had brought a game of horseshoes. Mr. Charlie was given a birthday beer and teamed up with Allie's dad. He still didn't know just quite what to say. One thing he did say a lot of was "sorry" when his shots rolled around and skinned ladies in the ankles. Kids whose parents had drug them along to the dance hall waltzed to the band. Some Boogers threw a football across the ponds. One of them tried to hold the team's place in line for dinner; he missed a pass that had to land in a lemon meringue pie.

Allie strolled around in Mr. Charlie's witch hat, proud of what she'd pulled off. She dropped a few firecrackers around the edges of it all for accents. After the major part of dinner she brought out a cake from under the bed and torched it up with all the candles she could find. Mr. Charlie held Butch in his arms and together they blew it all out.

Then it looked like things might be winding down. But, by now, you know better than that.

One person they hadn't heard much out of that night was Mrs. Avery. She and her husband had got there a little late after changing a flat tire. She walked around a little, listening to the Miserables and tapping her foot in the dirt. Then, for some unknown reason, she got inspired. After the music was over, she went over to the driveway alone, looked at the stars a little, took a swig of her cream soda and started to sing.

28.

Now, Mrs. Avery was sweet as peach cobbler. Which was what she had brought to the party for dessert; it was gone before the hot dogs even got warm. She also had an elevated post around Bernice, which explains the Mrs. part. She was the self-appointed visiting nurse for the whole town and most of the farms beyond it; she had a built-in sort of sickness radar, and when it picked up the slightest cough or complaint she came running with chicken soup and cherry pie (the pie was to keep everybody else in the house busy so the sick person had time to get well).

One thing it seemed she could not, absolutely could not do, was sing. Not for beans. In fact, there were certain kinds of beans that would have been offended by the comparison. She had joined the choir at church so long ago that people had forgotten when, or maybe they were trying to remember better days. She was tall and skinny as a street sign, and on her first Sunday morning (there were no rehearsals) she had stood above the rest of the choir in a gown that barely reached her kneecaps and let out an air raid siren of a sound. They sang three songs in a row that day, and the response from the congregation was more "oh my" than "amen."

The rest of the choir had waited – hid, really – behind the barbecue shack after church until she and her husband drove off. Then they found Pastor Walter and told him they were basically flipping out. Pastor Walter listened in a very compassionate manner, which is what pastors are trained to do, and then informed them that the church had to accommodate people of all callings and abilities. "Yeah," said Mr. Blackmon, "but she's calling something we don't want stampeding through the sanctuary."

But Mrs. Avery stayed on. After a while, it got to where the rest of the choir just stared over the tops of their hymnals at their shoes and sang "mrrmble, mrrmble." Their, or rather her, version of "Onward Christian Soldiers" made it seem to the congregation that, by the end, the war was pretty much right on top of them. Folks began to remember more and more distant family obligations that began early on Sunday morning. There started to be a lot more clattering in the offering plate than fluttering. Pastor Walter was a little worried. He had to keep the lights on; it was as simple as that. The more he prayed, however, the more the same message came back to him, albeit in nice italics with a pastel background: "Figure It Out."

Then he did, in fact, get an idea. He went out to the portable sign that sat on three legs and a tree stump in front of the church. This was where he usually put the title of next week's sermon or, if he didn't have one yet, a hunk of scripture or something he had found in a fortune cookie. He rearranged and added letters until it said:

"CHOIR WILL ONLY SING TWO SONGS THIS WEEK"

He stood back and looked at it, then put:

"FOR TIME REASONS"

That was kind of bending the truth, but hey, even the Bible says we are only put on this Earth for so long. Sort of.

The sign stayed that way for the rest of the year. Miraculously, or maybe understandably, nobody pointed it out. It was just enough for people to start sticking their toes back in the water. The first pews started to fill in a little, at least until folks could figure out the deadest part of the room acoustically and begin to pack in over there. Pastor Walter was preaching to left field, but the offering plate began to rustle again and Mrs. Avery never even noticed. She just stood up proud and tall and came as close to cracking the ceiling tiles as those two songs would allow. Of course, there had to be more music on Christmas and Easter, so for the whole shebangs Pastor Walter would have the crowd join in and sing. It got to be kinda funny, and sort of a challenge, trying to overpower Mrs. Avery on normally quiet songs like "Oh Holy Night" and "Away In A Manger," until it seemed the whole building was gonna rip loose from its foundation and blast into orbit. Most Sundays Skee and some of the other dogs, the real believers, stood around outside the front door howling their guts out, doing their best to provide the final ignition.

There also needed to be a little more preaching on a regular Sunday to fill in the full fifty minutes, but Pastor Walter just added to Children's Time with new stories including Laughing Leroy the Traveling Hebrew Ice Cream Man (the one where the freezer ran for eight days on just a day's worth of propane). And so the church went on as if it were a bighearted lion with a thorn in its paw, a kind, neighborly thorn who didn't appear to be able to carry a tune with a roomful of buckets.

But this one night (and, strangely, no time ever since) was different. Her voice, it seemed, had not been meant for the indoors. Probably not even for most kinds of outdoors, but tonight it was close to perfection. What struck people as amplified gargling in the church sanctuary sounded out here as if it was made by a gangly angel. With room to move, the notes floated across the ponds and among the lights like the sound of Oriental bells – still, though, some pretty big and gongy ones – and then did a peacock feathery roll down into the creek. Some of them landed on a bevy of bullfrogs, who joined in on the low parts. What fireflies there were gathered around her, lighting up her face and hair and turning her sunburned farmer husband, who had walked up beside her, into a grinning tomato.

Allie recognized the song she was singing. On rainy days at school, all the kids smashed into the gym to watch reels from old movies during recess. She had built up quite a list of films she had mostly seen. She had a lot of early attempts at horror films under her belt, and she sure could teach some of those guys a thing or two about playing dead.

But her favorites, the well-fudge-if-we-can't-play-outside kind of favorites, were the musicals. She loved how a guy would grab a girl around the waist and (just then, it seemed) figure out a reason to spin her up, down and through the most ridiculous situations you could imagine, all the while singing about his fluttering heart or something. It always made Allie smile.

This song was from "South Pacific," a movie that Allie liked, and it was called "Some Enchanted Evening." Mrs. Avery knew all the words by heart, which made Allie think it must've been special to her. Apparently it was special to a lot of the adult party guests, too, because they stopped cold and got these remembering looks on their faces. The children, who had moved across the road to look for dud fireworks or just about anything that would keep them away from the initial blast zone of Mrs. Avery's singing, came drifting back inside the gate.

They quietly sought out their parents, and if they couldn't find them they moved closer to Mrs. Avery in dust-covered little packs.

Allie, who had been conducting a tour of Goliath's pond for the really young ones, now stood watching Mr. Charlie across the driveway. He was looking at the fence and the road beyond it, but it seemed he wasn't thinking so much as remembering. Allie figured maybe he was remembering about the old movie house in Texarkana, how people would line up around the block to see the movie when it first came out, lining up to see what he, The Awfully Amazing Mr. Charlie, had to show them. Or maybe he was remembering about the war that was in the movie itself. The war he had gone off to fight only to find that it was all different, that for a lonely sailor stuck down in a ship, war was nowhere near what it was cracked up to be. Allie felt like he was definitely solving something. What it was soon became clear to her.

Mrs. Avery was wrapping up the song. The fireflies seemed to understand this, because they did a bunch of respectful little barrel rolls in front of her and took out across the ponds. The bullfrogs quieted down and flipped around in the creek, looking for their nine o'clock snacks. The adults began to clear their throats and dab at the corners of their eyes a little. A couple of the ladies, the really serious organizers, started doing the dishes again, rubbing the old gray forks and spoons and setting them down quietly.

Mr. Charlie had finished working stuff through in his mind and what came out as a result was a humongous surprise. Having seen "South Pacific" over and over again through his little projectionist's window – three times a day on weekends – he remembered the words just fine. He strolled over to Mrs. Avery to offer a little vocal support.

Mr. Charlie hadn't been to their church, so he didn't have the kind of anxiety some of the others did as he approached her; they winced a little, as if they were watching a volunteer from the audience prepare to put a circus lion through its paces. You didn't quite know what was gonna happen, but you felt it wasn't gonna be pretty. Not one bit.

But, in fact, it was kinda pretty. As you know, Mr. Charlie had a habit of humming to most every song that came through his radio. They were mostly what you call spirituals, or sometimes old country hits, but anyway he was quite a hummer. If he knew the words, or picked up the chorus while the song was going, he sang along in a voice that was not really classifiable; it was just what you would call agreeable. He stepped up next to Mrs. Avery and agreed with her on the last line:

"Once You Have Found Her, Never Let Her Go."

Mrs. Avery, who remember never paid attention to what the other choir members were doing at church, did this time. It wasn't that she had been challenged – although in her mind maybe she had a little – but more like complimented. She wasn't used to that at all. She stood a little taller, smiled at Mr. Charlie, and then sang the final line again just as it was meant to be:

"Once You Have Found Her, Never Let Her Go."

The song was finished. A couple of people coughed. Then they all applauded. Two or three of the guys wanted to give out a little "Whoop," but they let it pass. Mrs. Avery and her husband wandered back over; she pitched right in on the dishes, nodding to a couple of the ladies while Mr. Avery beamed at his friends as if one of his chickens had just won some sort of a ribbon.

Mr. Charlie had walked the other way, over to the shed and the goldfish food. He leaned against the corner of the shed for a minute, looking over the Ambolini's graves. Then he turned and headed back to the party. He and Allie caught each other's eyes. In them, she was saying "Happy Birthday, Mr. Charlie." And, in his, he was saying "Thank You, Allie. For Everything."

29.

The next day was clear and blue. And not quite so hot. Allie slept a little late. She threw on some shorts and one of her new beach shirts; it mentioned something about margaritas, but her mom had let it slide.

When she got there, it looked like he was gone again. His car was there though. It had a kind of a form fitting tarp over it that was riddled with prehistoric bird splatter. Allie put away some leftover dishes and started some coffee for when he got back. Then she saw a note on the table.

"Dear Allie,

The bus leaves for Houston in the middle of the night, so I don't think I should wake you.

From there I have to get on another train. It will be a long ride and I don't know when else I can tell you all of this. So I have to tell you now.

Love, Allie. Love and longing. One part keeps us grounded and the other keeps us searching. I could sure stay here and play fish with you and your brother until the end of my days. But there's something always in me that says I gotta go.

I am going to try to find Miss Rebecca. Goodness knows I won't ever do it, or what sort of stuff she will have going on if I do. But while I can still read bus schedules and write letters, and while there's still some money in the bank, I gotta try. I will miss you and your friends a lot, and your parents and all of them. Thank everyone for the party too. I know you had a lot to do with it. That's what finally got me going.

Strikes me that I never settled up with you. For a while I've been thinking about the right way to do that. In a few days, go see Mrs. Horner the lawyer downtown with your folks. She will have the signal from me to put it all into something called a trust for you. That way it will be yours. The ponds and the fish and all of it. Someday you may think I really saddled you with a project, but that's all it's ever been and I think you can handle it. You have handled it before.

Well, like I said, I gotta go.

Your Pal,

Charlie

P.S. Take good care of the car. I guess it will be yours too. It has helped me through some times. And Goliath. Also your stick is still in the closet for when you need it."

She had to sit down of course. She thought for a minute about it and then she started to sniff a little. Then she looked across the table and started to cry. There were the scissors, up against some old hair wrapped up tight. Mr. Charlie was telling her, at last, he belonged. Even though he had taken off on his own once again, he belonged.

Allie took up the scissors through the tears. She went into the bathroom. In the part of the mirror you could still see through, she took hers off too. She carried it in and wrapped it up with his. She hid them in an old box of tea bags in the top of the cupboard. Then she sat down and kept on crying.

There is one more word you need to know. The word is pahook. You won't find it anywhere either, but it's important. That's because you have to stop crying sometime, and hopefully soon. You'll think of something to lean on in your mind, and that will help you catch your breath. Then out pops pahook.

What got her pahooking was Skee. He had wormed his way in and was lying on his back for a good patting down. He had a goofy smile on his face like he knew just what he was doing. That's what Allie leaned on. She reached over and rubbed his tummy some. Then she switched off the stove, picked up Mr. Charlie's note and went outside into the sun.

She walked over to Fnorrt and pulled off one of the new grips. She rolled the note up and stuffed it in the handlebars. Skee was sitting by the picnic bench, taking in the scenery and still smiling. Allie sat down and rubbed him some more under the chin. Then she smiled too. There was still plenty of day left, and for that matter a little of the summer.

She thought about riding out to Candy's to see how the pigs were doing. Or maybe she should just go home and write some of it down. New legends were already brewing in her head. But she had something to do first. It was time to feed the goldfish.

Made in the USA
Charleston, SC
15 January 2017